Norma Jean Lutz Classic Collection

Flower in the Hills

Norma Jean Lutz

Flower in The Hills

ISBN: 978-0-9859571-7-9

Copyright © 2014 by NUWSLink, Inc. and Norma Jean Lutz.

Except for use in any review, the reproduction or utilization of this work in whole or in part in any form by any electronic, mechanical, or other means, now known or hereafter invented is forbidden without the permission of the publisher, NUWSLink, Inc., 8703-R North Owasso Expressway, Ste. 143, Owasso, OK 74055

A Word about the
Norma Jean Lutz Classic Collection

During my writing career I have been privileged to have over 50 titles published under my name. Due to the nature of the publishing world in days past, most of these titles were off the shelves and out of print in a short period of time. Sad but true.

Now, a new day has dawned in the world of publishing. Digital publishing and independent publishing have created the opportunity for my past titles to be reintroduced to a whole new generation of readers.

These stories are timeless in spite of the fact they were penned several decades ago. Hence, I have chosen to call them the *Norma Jean Lutz Classic Collection.*

I'm excited to be able to bring these stories out of the files and into your hands. I hope you enjoy your read.

Norma Jean Lutz

PS: *Flower in the Hills* is the first title in the *Classic Collection*—with many more to follow.

NOTE FROM THE AUTHOR

I first wrote *Flower in the Hills* in the 1980s. This version is taken from the original manuscript, the only changes being minor edits.

Living in Oklahoma, I'm only a short drive from the Ozarks and I visit there often. Years ago, I suffered from the miserable malady of car sickness, thus it was easy to imagine Latina's queasiness as she experiences the hills for the first time.

Here's hoping you enjoy this *Norma Jean Lutz Classic Collection* selection.

Norma Jean Lutz

A note from the author:
I love to hear from my readers. You may contact me here:
NormaJean@BeANovelist.com
http://www.CleanTeenReads.net
http://www.normajeanlutz.com

Cover Photo Credit
http://www.dreamstime.com/
white-flower-stock-photo-imagefree113790

This book is dedicated to:

Kerry, Mary, and Tobias Vincent Lutz
With my deepest, heartfelt love

ACKNOWLEDGEMENTS

In appreciation to those of you who have served—and indeed are still serving—as my cheerleaders, boosters, supporters, and encouragers. The only thing better than having a dream, is to have others who also believe in your dream. Many thanks to each and every one of you.

Will and Rhonda Huber
Kerry and Mary Lutz
Zach Clark
Gerry and Sadia Blaksley
Glenn and Ami Shaffer
DestinyLifeChurch.TV
Mike and Katie Baker
Dan and Elva Fellers
Mike and Anita Welch
Jeremy and Annie Donovan
John and Robbyn Bartley
John Cunningham, Jr.
Caleb and Natasha Mitchell

Jeff and Lynne' Ray
Craig and Margie Day
Judy Keefe
Dusty and Terri Smith
Chris and Charity Tankersley
Coy and Nickki Burton
Betsy Cisco
Randye Sharp
Daniel and Kendra Muilenburg
Judith Miller
Richard and Sarah Ade Lodato
Chad and Ali Quisenberry

CHAPTER ONE

L atina Harmen knew she was going to hate Missouri. "There's nothing in Missouri!" she had told her father when he announced they were to spend the summer there. And now she knew she'd been one hundred and ten percent right.

The Harmen's family car lurched and swayed around each sharp hairpin curve deep in the green-black Ozark Mountains. As the dense stands of trees flew by, Latina had been watching the curving roads and valleys directly beneath the road they were on. But now she was unable to look out the window at all.

The usually sweet fragrance of her father's pipe was making her feel sick. She pressed her forehead against the cool window and squeezed her eyes shut. She couldn't have motion sickness. Latina, the girl who fearlessly rode the wildest rides at the oceanfront park in Periwinkle Cove each and every summer? Impossible.

Her thirteen-year-old brother, Dirk, had finally stopped his nerve-shattering habit of snapping the little rubber bands on his braces and was now gazing out his window at the panoramic view, offering a few intelligent comments such as, "Wow!" and "Gee whiz, would you look at that."

His very excitement over this desolate place was more than enough to nauseate Latina even without the constant, unending rocking of the car.

She clenched her teeth in a determined effort not to be sick in the car like a little kid. As she did, a soft uncontrollable moan escaped her lips.

Dirk turned to look at her. "Hey Mom! Latina's making like Casper the Ghost."

In a sort of haze, she heard her mother saying to her father, "Oh, Ross! She's car sick. How much farther?"

"We turn off the main highway about five miles up ahead, but then it's seven more miles to Zell's Bush."

Her mother looked around at her again, her face filled with concern. "Think you can hold on that long, Latina?"

Latina nodded without unclenching her teeth. The hamburger she'd had for lunch felt as it were hanging somewhere in the halfway spot of her esophagus.

Zell's Bush. Even the name of the town to which they were headed was revolting. Every new lurch of the car took her farther and farther from the beach at Periwinkle Cove. And from Kent Starner.

As far as she could see out across the valleys, there were hills of deep green pine, which looked almost black—black and ominous. It seemed like an eternity before they turned a tight little curve on the dusty back road and saw a huddle of buildings sitting just past a sign announcing: *Zell's Bush. POP 381.*

Her father parked the car, jumped out, and took long strides up the wooden step to the high porch of a store whose faded sign read *Boles' Grocery.* Within minutes he called out to his wife to bring Latina inside.

When Latina thought back to it later, there wasn't much she could remember about being led into the back living quarters of the dusty old store. Her stomach was kinked in little knots and her hair felt pasted to her head.

An old bathtub stood upon four quaint claw legs and the pipes came out of holes in the wooden floor to the faucets. She recalled sitting on the edge of that old tub while her mother held a cold cloth to her burning forehead. Voices coming from the store drifted back to them as Latina sat there attempting to regain her composure after having lost all her lunch.

She heard an older man saying, "I'm Orville Boles, and this here's my wife, Maude. You folks heading for the Nettle ton place?"

"No," she could hear her father explain in his patient professor voice. "We're looking for the farm that Professor Kirkland owns. He's a friend of mine. He's in Europe for the summer, so we're renting it."

"Yep. That there's the one. It's the Nettleton place. The Nettletons owned it nigh on to fifty years."

When Latina emerged from the back room with her mother, Mr. Boles was drawing her father a map on a brown paper bag that showed how to get to the farm. Thin, frail Maude Boles smiled at her sympathetically and made a *tsking* sound through her dentures. Latina looked away, wishing someone would offer her a place to sit down.

It wasn't until that very moment that she noticed the young man sitting in a straight-backed chair tipped against the wall next to the pop cooler. His arms were folded across his broad chest and his long legs allowed his feet to remain flat on the floor. A shock of sandy curls lay across his forehead and his dancing blue eyes were laughing at her.

"Let's go back to the car, Mom," she whispered as her hand flew to her mussed and matted hair.

"We can wait till you're feeling a little better," her mother suggested. "No need to hurry now. We're almost there."

A few minutes earlier, Latina had never wanted to ride in a car ever again, but now she said. "Let's go to the car *now*, Mother. Please!"

She couldn't bear those laughing eyes on her another second.

The screen door was held by a snaky-looking long black spring that made the door bang shut as they went out.

Her father and Dirk followed shortly, chattering about their first glimpse of Zell's Bush. "Paulie," the professor said, "did you ever see the likes of that store? Just like a scene from Ma and Pa Kettle wasn't it?"

"Somewhat, I suppose." Her mother's voice was non committal.

"That tall guy was really cool," Dirk was saying in his usual breathless way. "Did you see the muscles on that dude? What'd they say his name was, Dad?"

"Clouse. Tully Clouse, I think. They drawl their words so that I can barely make out what they're saying."

Clouse! Latina seethed inwardly. Should have been *Louse*. That clod, who looked like he was wearing his little brother's jeans, had laughed at her! As if coming to this miserable place and then getting sick weren't degrading enough, that hillbilly had had the audacity to laugh at her.

Gray clouds gathered in the sky as they traveled the winding road from Boles' Grocery to the farm. Twice, their car bumped over metal bridges that rattled beneath them in protest. Her mother remarked that the road must wind and turn more than the streams did.

Latina mutely agreed.

The fact that the two-story farmhouse was in better repair than Latina thought it might be did nothing to cheer her. It was nothing in comparison to their charming cottage at the cove on the East Coast where they had stayed every summer for as long as she could remember.

A few drops of rain had begun to fall as her father brought the last of their luggage into the cavernous house. After the long tedious hours traveling from their home in Eagleton, Ohio, Dirk now exploded into a missile, shooting from room to room. His insatiable curiosity about the big old house made it impossible for their father to get any help out of him.

Dirk reported that there were four *humongous* bedrooms upstairs and immediately staked his claim on the southeast room that overlooked the meandering driveway and the expanse of the valley. He wanted to see the sun come up, the announced to all who would listen as he leaned precariously over the balcony railing at the head of the stairs.

The musty smells of the old house—which had recently been opened up and aired out by one of the local women—didn't do much for Latina's queasy stomach.

"As soon as I locate the teakettle, Latina," her mother said as they carried boxes into the kitchen, "I'll heat you some soup and make a cup of tea."

Latina set the box she was carrying on the kitchen table which was spread with a worn, flower-print oilcloth. She watched as her mother gazed about the room. "This place smells like my Grandma's old farmhouse."

The statement surprised Latina. She hadn't heard her mother speak much about her family, all of whom had lived in Kansas and had long since passed away before Latina was born.

The air in the house was cool and clammy. As soon as Latina located the right suitcase, she pulled out her bulky blue cardigan and slipped its warmth over her bare arms. She then grabbed her transistor radio from the same suitcase and tuned in her favorite music to chase the formidable silence out of the house.

Now raindrops pelted more persistently. Her father planted his tall frame before a window in the front room and looked out across the wide front porch. He tamped his unlit pipe with his forefinger. "It's a bit cool," he commented. "Wonder if we could find enough dry wood to start a fire."

The room was flanked on the north by a massive stone fireplace situated between two bay windows.

Dirk was banging out a painful rendition of "Peter, Peter, Pumpkin Eater" on an old upright piano he had discovered. Hitting a final note, he jumped up at his father's suggestion. "All right! Lead me to the woodpile. I brought my trusty hatchet."

Latina marveled at the two of them as they walked into the deepening darkness as though it were their well-lit yard in Eagleton. Although she knew her mother needed help in the kitchen, Latina sank into one of the overstuffed chairs in front of the fireplace and closed her eyes.

Presently, her father and Dirk brought in some sickly looking sticks of wood and made an effort to start a fire. "Jim told me about the remodeling they'd done on this place," her father was saying, his head inside the fireplace's black cavity. "He seemed to be particularly proud of this fireplace." He placed the kindling on top of pieces of wadded up newspapers. "I can see why now. This is a beaut."

Good old Professor Kirkland, Latina thought. She wished he'd never come on staff at Eagleton State College where her father was dean of the history department. That way they would never have heard of Zell's Bush, Missouri. She thought again of that awful moment at supper two weeks ago when her father had announced to the family that they were not going to the cove for the summer. Latina had nearly choked.

"Your mother and I have been discussing this off and on for some time," he told them in his slow, methodical way. "As you know, the cove has become increasingly crowded and commercialized each year. It's not the quiet summer retreat it once was. Now it's glutted with disco dance joints, pawn shops, bars, and tourist traps everywhere. I'm finding it more and more difficult to complete the research I set out to do each summer. Not enough peace and quiet."

Latina had sat there frozen as she heard about Jim Kirkland's sabbatical in Europe and his offer to rent out the quiet farm in the Ozarks. "And I've decided to take him up on his offer," her dad said with finality.

The commercialization, as her father called it, consisted of wonderful fun places to be. Especially the dinner club with a dance floor out over the sparkling water where she and Kent Starner danced in a dream world last summer.

A few days ago, before they left Eagleton, she'd received a note from Kent explaining that he would be in Mexico for a week at the beginning of the summer, but then would be meeting her again at Periwinkle Cover later in June. Painfully, she wrote back to explain to him of her sudden change of plans, and gave him the Zell's Bush address.

Latina turned toward what was left of the dying fire. She could see Dirk's initial excitement over the prospect of a glowing fire was waning. The wood they had found was too wet. "What are we going to do tonight with no television?" His voice was flat.

Latina sank further back into the chair. "Let me stay in Eagleton with Grandma Stanton and get a job," she had begged her mother privately in her room after hearing her father's news. "At least I'll be with my friends all summer."

But her mother shook her head. "Next year you'll be graduating, Latina. Let's let this be a together-summer for our family. We'll have a different kind of good time. You'll see."

Latina had seen all she wanted to see of this *different kind of good time*. The chill of the room permeated her very bones.

Her father leaned back on his heels where he sat crouched in front of the fireplace. Weariness was taking the edge off his enthusiasm as well. He sighed. "It'd be best for all of us, I suppose, to go to bed early tonight. We're all exhausted from the trip."

"To bed?" Dirk's groan of disbelief was followed by a call from their mother in the kitchen.

The three of them were thankful to see the kitchen table set about with thick ham sandwiches and mugs of steaming tea. Pauline had closed off the kitchen doors and the gas cooking stove's oven door was open, warming the room.

Latina's father laughed. "Paulie, you outsmarted these two Boy Scouts in getting a fire started." He gave his wife a grateful hug while Dirk plowed into his sandwich.

Latina chose to sip alternately from her steaming tea, then her bowl of soup, letting the warmth trickle down to her insides.

"What a blessing," her mother said, "that the Kirklands called ahead to have a lady open the house for us." She rubbed her fingers across the oilcloth thoughtfully. "I think they said her name was Garwood."

"Garwood?" Dirk's interest was suddenly sparked. "I saw a sign just up from the grocery store that said, *Garwood's Sawmill.* Maybe that's where the lady lives.

"I don't know, son." The professor leaned back in his chair and lit his after-dinner pipe. "In such a small town, everyone is related to everyone else. There could be fifty families of Garwoods."

I doubt there are fifty families in the whole county," Latina commented dryly. She hadn't meant it as a joke, but everyone laughed.

Latina thought of her best friend, Camille Dawson, who was leaving to spend two weeks in the Bahamas. Before school was out, the two of them talked often of the awesome tans they would have next fall as they began their senior year together at Eagleton High. Now the thought of Cammie lying on the deck of a luxurious cruise ship while she sat in the kitchen of a dank old farmhouse was unbearable. How could her parent have done this to her?

"The screened-in porch is perfect to catch the afternoon sun," her mother was saying in an irritatingly casual voice. "I think I'll put some hanging planters out there."

Her mother, who at first seemed to be Latina's only ally, was sounding terribly settled in. It was worrisome for Latina, who was now dreading going up the stairs into the darkened bedroom.

Her parents had chosen the east bedroom adjacent to Dirk's and her father mentioned that he preferred the room overlooking the backyard for his study. The room adjoining the study was the one left for Latina.

The wind came up and whistled in the windows as Latina scurried quickly into the strange bed. Her radio lay on the pillow next to her ear, but the rattling windows gave stiff competition to its soothing sounds.

She fumbled with the dial on the transistor before realizing that the batteries had given out. She was such a dummy. Why hadn't she thought to replace them?

It was a wretched beginning to what she knew was going to be a wretched summer.

CHAPTER TWO

When footsteps on the creaking stairs awakened her the next morning, sunlight was streaming in the tall windows. Her father passed by her door carrying a box loaded with his typewriter and several books.

Seeing she was awake, he paused at her door. "Good morning, Latina. We decided to let you sleep and get over your jet lag." He chuckled at his own joke.

"Thanks a bunch," she answered. His silly grin drew a reluctant smile from her.

It was comfortable to lie there and listen to the busy noises her father made in the adjoining room. In the morning light, looking out on the jade-green, freshly rain-washed backyard, she almost had to admit this was a good place for him to study. Lazily, she got out of bed, pulled on her robe and headed downstairs.

Her mother was puttering in the kitchen. "This place has such a homey atmosphere, doesn't it," she said.

Latina's answer was a noncommittal grunt. She had several adjectives that weren't as flattering as "homey," but obviously this wasn't the time to express them. Absently, she poured a bowl of corn flakes into a bowl and considered whether to eat a piece of cold bacon.

She thought of Cammie on her way to the Bahamas this very minute. Obviously, she would be staying at one of the most exclusive hotels. And perhaps Kent had already arrived in Mexico. Hopefully, he would write soon.

Leaving half of the soggy cereal, she walked out to the screened-in porch off the kitchen and shivered as the rain-cooled breeze touched her face. She moved past green metal lawn chairs with chipped paint, out the screen door and down the stone steps, walking barefoot onto the wet grass.

She could hear Dirk thrashing around in the tumble-down barn off to her right. He had already discovered some rusty horseshoes and had asked his mother for permission to take them back to Eagleton. He appeared to be entranced by this so-called farm and the "swallowing-up" hills as he had so aptly named them.

"They're swallowing us up," he had muttered as he gazed out the car window at the ebony hills on their trip down. To Latina, the thought was about as appealing as Jonah's experience in the belly of the big fish. Lucky Jonah. His confinement lasted three short days; hers was three eternal months.

"Want some help unpacking, dear?" her mother asked as Latina stood at the back door drying her wet feet on an old towel.

"No thanks," she replied. "I think I can handle it." Slowly she made her way up to her room to work.

Later, after lunch, her father suggested they drive down to Boles' and ask Mr. Boles where they might buy firewood. "If we locate some," he said, "we'll stack it on the porch so it'll be handy for cool evenings."

"Are there going to be many more cool evenings?" Latina wanted to know.

"Well, let's face it. It won't be quite as balmy as Periwinkle Cove."

Latina thought of brilliant sunshine on sparkling white sand and pulled her cardigan more snugly about her.

"If we're going to the grocery store, I can get BBs for my gun." Dirk was eager to get out in the woods and shoot off his gun.

Latina hoped Boles' Grocery was *uptown* enough to have the type of batteries she needed for her transistor, but this turned out to be a vain hope.

Orville Boles was in no hurry to get up from his chair behind the small checkout counter. But he stretched forth a leathery hand to grasp the professor's and gave a cheery, "Howdy! What can I do for you?"

"We need firewood, Mr. Boles, to take the edge off the nippy evenings. Know where we can get some?"

"It has been a mite cooler this spring. You might need a couple ricks of wood at that." The words came out of the old man as though churned out slowly by a crank.

Latina searched for batteries. Mrs. Boles appeared from nowhere and patted her shoulder with a thin, blue-veined hand. "How are you today, dearie?"

Latina drew back from her touch. "I'm fine, thank you." Showing the dead battery in her hand to Mrs. Boles, Latina heard Mr. Boles tell her father to check at Garwood's Sawmill for firewood, which he pronounced *farwood.*

"We saw that sign at the turnoff," he father commented. "They have firewood do they?"

"Nope just lumber." Mr. Boles fell silent.

Latina's father waited.

Presently the old man clumped his chair down on its four legs with a bang. "That young feller you met yesterday,

Tully Clouse. He works there. For a little extra money, he'll cut tops for you and carry 'em to you in his pickup."

Meanwhile, as Latina waited, Mrs. Boles slowly fingered through battery packages gritty with dust, looking closely to make out each label. After a long time, she turned back to Latina. "We don't have such a one as that," she said squinting. "Sorry."

As Latina made her way to the front of the store her father was saying, "Thanks, Orville. We'll stop by the mill on our way home. Say, Pauline and Dirk have a couple of items here we need to pay for."

"Maude!" Mr. Boles called out without moving, "you got a couple of customers here."

Latina slipped the lifeless battery into her jeans pocket and stepped out onto the dilapidated wood porch that fronted the store. The miniature main street was, to her, like a cartoon from a joke book—a small, littered gas station; a cement-block bank building painted a dull brown; and Boles' store. Not even a pizza place, she thought wistfully. It was like visiting another country.

"Clouse did odd jobs for them other folks what lived up at the Nettleton place," she heard Mr. Boles saying. "He's a dandy worker."

As she climbed into their car, Latina hoped that the *dandy worker* would not be doing any work at their house. How much worse could the summer get?

Turning off the main road at the sign, her father drove a short distance before reaching the mill operation which was situated on a level clearing in a low-lying valley.

Lurching down the rutted drive, they met a semi-trailer heavily loaded with cut lumber, grinding its gears as it slowly made its way up from the mill. Her father was forced to pull off the drive to let it pass. The driver waved and grinned. Her father returned the wave, then drove on toward a graveled area where several other vehicles were parked.

As Latina got out of the car, she was greeted by the warm fragrance of cut wood and the shrill screams of the saws that were housed in open-sided sheds. Metal chains clanked harshly as workers loosened them to unload freshly cut logs from a trailer bed.

A bear of a man came striding toward them with a large hand outstretched to the professor. "Howdy folks. I'm Parke Garwood. Looking for something? How can I help?"

Her father introduced the family, explained where they were staying for the summer and added that Orville Boles told them of the possibility of getting firewood.

"Clouse does that," Mr. Garwood said, pointing to the sheds. "He's right here. Let's go ask him." To Pauline, he said, "Why don't you women-folk head on up to the house." He waved toward a winding pathway that led to a small house tucked up against the side of the hill. "Just knock at the door. I'm of a mind that Etta Ann still has some coffee hot."

It irritated Latina to be referred to as "women-folk" and to be told what to do by this stranger. As her mother thanked him and made her way up the path, Latina deliberately held back and strolled the other way. When her mother glanced back, Latina shook her head.

She wanted no part of that house. This place reminded her of the nursery rhyme of the crooked little man with the crooked little house. How she longed for the straight, square, named streets of Eagleton.

Dirk had discovered the mountain of sawdust behind the sheds and was investigating. Latina had already noticed

Tully working under the open shed along with several other men. His broad-shouldered frame was unmistakable. She watched as her father talked to Tully, and she wondered if the workers were laughing at them for wanting firewood in the summer.

As she turned to walk back to the car, she noticed several hand-carved figurines on a ledge of the shed nearest her. Giving in to her curiosity, she stepped over to have a closer look. The miniature works of art were polished to a high sheen. Several were of animals—squirrels and raccoons—but one that especially interested her was of a little girl. She picked it up to study the intricate details. The girl's head was cocked to one side like a tiny bird listening for dangers in the forest.

"Well, would you looky here." A voice startled her. "Last night's spring rain done brought a blossom to the hills."

Latina turned to look into the face of a dark-eyed young man with straight black hair. Slowly she replaced the figurine.

"I'm Collier Hunsecker, and this here's my cousin, Tully Clouse," he said.

Beside him, towering nearly a head taller, stood Tully. Once again she was looking into the lively blue eyes that were twinkling in laughter at her.

"And what might your name be?" Collier asked as he filled a cup from a large metal water cooler.

"Her name is Latina," ventured Tully in an even tone. "I heard them say yesterday over at Boles'."

"Sounds purty as a flower, don't it?" Collier's dark eyes studied her over the rim of the metal cup. "Latina." He reached over to touch her dark hair that lay over her shoulder. She stepped back with a sudden start.

"When I first saw this flower," Tully put in, "a drive through the hills had rather wilted it." His drawl seemed less pronounced than his cousin's.

"Wilted, huh?" Collier retorted. "That little Latina-flower? It sure come back to life, now didn't it?"

Latina didn't intend to stand there and be talked about as though she were a botanical specimen. "I came back to life, all right," she said. "Because I'm of the highly resistant variety!" Whirling about, she hastily retreated to the safety of the car and slammed the door on their laughter. She pretended to be reading something in her lap and hoped they couldn't see it was a road map. How she wished her parents would hurry and take her away from this awful place.

Just then, a tall, slender girl in faded jeans and a worn print blouse came down the path from the house. She approached smiling and motioned for Latina to roll down her window.

"Howdy," she said breathlessly. "I'm Donna Dee Garwood. I didn't know till this very minute that you were out here, or I'd have come out to meet you sooner. Your mama just now mentioned that you were out here alone. Welcome to Zell's Bush. We're so glad to have you."

The drawl of her words didn't seem so repulsive coming from this girl. Her welcome sounded genuine—a salve to Latina's wounded ego.

"I guess this place is pretty different from what you're used to, huh?"

"That's an understatement." Quickly, Latina added, "I guess I'm just not used to these hills. Uh, the closeness of them." She was fumbling because honestly she didn't know for sure what it was she didn't like. It was as if hidden danger lurked in the dense trees. The thick hills were ominous and foreboding.

"You'll get used to them and come to love them," the girl replied. "I work in Palatka and I'm not home much, but I'd be glad to take you there next Saturday to do some shopping or just fool around."

Latina remembered driving through Palatka. It wasn't much bigger than Zell's Bush and nothing like Eagleton, but the friendly spirit in which the invitation was offered spurred her to accept with a degree of graciousness.

As they discussed their plans, her parents came down the path followed by Mr. Garwood and his wife, Etta Ann.

"You shoulda come on up to the house with your mama," Etta Ann said after introductions had been made. "No need of you sitting out here like a scared rabbit. When you come back, you come on in like you're one of us. Y'hear?"

Latina nodded and smiled.

As they bumped out of the deeply rutted driveway, Latina marveled at the Garwoods' friendliness. She had imagined these people would resent intruders coming in.

Her father was talking excitedly about Mr. Garwood's aging father, known as Old Man Gar, who lived alone up in the hills. Parke felt the elderly man might open his storehouse of bygone memories and stories about the original settling of Zell's Bush.

"I think I've hit upon a new research project, Pauline." The professor's voice was laced with childlike enthusiasm. "Maybe enough for a book—about these people and their ancestors, and their way of life up here."

"A book?" Pauline reached over and patted her husband's shoulder tenderly. "How wonderful, Ross. Sounds like a marvelous opportunity."

Latina was uncomfortable amidst all this good news. As the car careened up the hills, she attempted to peer through the thick forest, but she couldn't see past the dense growth of trees. Somehow, she had expected the people in the town to be just as closed as the forest, but they weren't.

Donna Dee might very well be the saving grace of her summer. Meeting her had been a respite after the run-in with those two overgrown louts. Now she had something to look forward to—next Saturday with Donna Dee.

CHAPTER THREE

Latina's father had the foresight to load a few logs in the trunk while at the sawmill, since Tully wouldn't make a delivery until the next day. The orange glow of the flames in the stone fireplace that evening, accompanied by intermittent pops and snaps, transformed the living room into a more cozy setting.

Sitting in the arm chair nearest the fire, Latina watched as her father rummaged through the bookshelves that lined the west wall. "Hey, Dirk," he said reaching down to a low shelf. "Look. Board games." Immediately he challenged Dirk to a game of Scrabble.

Just then Pauline came into the room with skeins of yarn, crochet hooks and a magazine full of patterns. Latina was surprised. Her mother hadn't done handiwork for years and had said she didn't care about it anymore. Actually, she'd had little time since she'd gone back to teaching freshman composition at the college this past year.

Pauline settled into the other chair in front of the fire and soon the crochet hook was threading in and out, carrying with it the trail of variegated pastels of yarn.

Latina wanted to scream. Everyone seemed so disgustingly contented. Restlessly, she got up and walked over to the bay windows and looked out. There were no streetlights, no yard lights, no house lights, no hint of any other living thing on the other side of the glass. Only her sad reflection staring back at her.

In their letters through the winter, she and Kent had talked about this being the best summer of their entire lives. When he first noticed her last year, it had been like a dream come true. They'd met at the drugstore, which was the hangout for all the kids who regularly spent summers at the cove. Soon Kent was coming by the cottage nearly every day to take her swimming, picnicking, sailing on his father's boat, or dancing in the evenings. There had been an air of assuredness about him so lacking in other guys she knew. Tall, tan and very blond, Kent always turned heads in a crowd. She was proud to be by his side.

Sometimes they went off from the others and walked down the beach hand-in-hand, out to the rugged, rocky point. It became a special place for them. It was there, at the point, where he first held her close, kissed her, and told her he loved her.

Perhaps her parents had changed their summer plans because they thought she was getting too serious about Kent. The recurring thought gnawed at her insides. If that were true, they were making a terrible mistake. She would never forget Kent. Never! And she was sure he'd be coming to visit her on his way home from Mexico. Then everyone would see how important it was that they be together.

She turned from her reflection in the window to the bookshelves. Professor Kirkland had stocked them well. She flipped through the pages of a couple books before selecting a mystery. She planned to lose herself in the book.

The plot was mediocre at best, and Latina hadn't realized until she was nearly half finished that it was having a morbid effect on her. Later, after everyone had settled in bed for the night, the silence in her room became more oppressive than before. Branches scratched against the windows and the wind whipped the clouds past the moon. She struggled to stifle her fears; half hoping her mother might come to quell them. But no one came.

When the morning sun streamed in her window, Latina sat upright and shook off the moroseness of the previous evening. She jumped out of bed, reached for her robe, and ran down to the kitchen. Grabbing the bacon from the fridge, she laid strips out in neat rows in the large cast iron skillet. The clatter of setting the table and the cooking smells soon woke the family.

Within the hour, they were chatting good-naturedly around the table, teasing Latina, asking why she hadn't gotten up earlier and why she hadn't fixed at least a dozen more fried eggs. She laughed along with them, determined that she would not let this place get the best of her. Somehow she needed to find something to do. She could simply sit around and rot.

Her father and Dirk announced that they were taking a hike through the valley toward Zell's Bush. Her mother said perhaps on another day she might join them, but she wasn't settled in enough to go running off. Visions of snakes, lizards, and scorpions slithering under rocks and dead logs prompted Latina's refusal of their invitation.

Later, as she moved about the house, she tried to envision the younger Kirkland children running about playing games of tag and make believe in the big house. Before Kent came into her life, she too could have been swept up in the novelty of such an out-of-the-way place. But he had changed the way she looked at everything around her, and Zell's Bush was just a boring old hillbilly town stuck out in the middle of nowhere.

By midmorning, all her good intentions had drained away. Listlessly, she followed the sounds of hammering out in the kitchen where her mother was hanging wall plaques. Dutifully, Latina offered her assistance. As she handed her mother the hammer or nails when asked, he mind floated away again to where the kids at Periwinkle Cove would be shouting as they ran into the foamy breakers, or as they lay tanning in the warm sun.

"Latina? You asleep?"

"Huh?"

"I said, would you please go down to the road and get the mail? I thought I heard the mailman's car go by a while ago."

"Sorry. I was lost in thought. Sure," she said, laying the hammer on the table, "I'll go."

"And what choice do I have?" she muttered as she pushed open the front door. "The highlight of my day—take a trip down the driveway to the mailbox. Lucky me."

As she was walking back up the drive carrying a few pieces of unimportant mail forwarded to them from Eagleton, she heard the rattle of an approaching vehicle. Not many people traveled this road. It slowed at the end of the drive and turned in. Glancing over her shoulder, she saw a battered blue pickup coming up the drive. It was Tully delivering the wood. As she stepped from the gravel drive onto the grass, the pickup stopped beside her.

"Ride to the house?" he called over the noise of the clattering motor.

"I need the exercise, thank you." Her words were clipped.

"Suit yourself." He gave a nod and a half-smile, shifted gears, and drove on. Little rocks spit out from the tires, hitting her bare legs. She glowered at the pickup as it moved behind the house where the wood was to be stacked inside the screened-in porch.

How much wood could they need? At the cove she would have been wearing her swim suit most every day. Now, dressed in a cotton blouse and a pair of shorts, she shivered as she walked beneath the shade of the towering oaks.

Placing the mail on the piano in the front room, she browsed through the bookshelves again. Oh for a boring television rerun or something! Anything!

Noises from the kitchen indicated Pauline was still puttering. Latina couldn't fathom how her mother could enjoy such a decrepit kitchen that was paltry in comparison to theirs back home.

"Latina? Come here a minute, please."

As Latina slowly entered the kitchen, her mother was handing her a tall glass of iced water. "Here. Take this to our hard-working young man out there." She nodded to where Tully was unloading wood from the bed of the pickup.

Why doesn't she just hand it to him herself, Latina wondered. Through the door she watched Tully work. Each move was calculated and measured. His thick sandy-brown hair fell carelessly across his forehead.

As she opened the screen door leading from the kitchen, he turned toward her and flashed a wide smile. "Howdy," he said, as if he hadn't seen her just a few minutes ago out front.

"Mother thought you looked hot and thirsty," she said. "She asked me to bring this out." It sounded redundant. Almost childish.

"I'm obliged to your mother. She's mighty thoughtful." Amusement shone in his eyes.

He's laughing at me again, she thought. Why did this country bumpkin continually put her on the defensive? She turned to go.

"Say, there's a wood tick there on your leg," he said softly. His voice had a husky quality about it.

He was probably kidding. She'd play it cool and not look down or panic.

"I can get it off for you real simple."

Still she stood there wondering how best to call his bluff.

"If you pull it off and leave the head in, it could give you some bad trouble," he continued in the same soft tone.

A gasp escaped from her when she looked down at the tiny creature buried in her skin just above her knee. How she detested crawling things. She restrained a scream.

He stepped toward her and placed his large hands on her arms and gently guided her to one of the metal lawn chairs nearest her. She felt the icy metal touch the backs of her legs.

He knelt down before her on the splintery porch floor. His sandy hair was very close to her face. She felt she couldn't breathe.

Deftly, he took hold of the insect in the tips of his fingernails and began to turn it around. Once it slipped from his grasp and he patiently took hold again and continued turning it around. "Clockwise," he explained, "so's they'll let go." He looked up momentarily and she was looking full into his clear blue eyes.

She wanted to push him away. It was all his fault. If he hadn't run her off the driveway into the grass, she wouldn't even have a tick on her leg.

"This won't be the last of the pesky fellows you'll meet up with. Just remember to turn them clockwise and they'll let loose." As he said the words, the insect released itself into his fingers.

"Want to see him?"

"Get it away from me." Her voice was sharp.

He pinched it with his fingernails, calmly rose, and dropped it outside the screen door on the grass.

"I guess I should thank you," she said coolly, struggling for self possession.

"Mercy no, ma'am," he retorted. "I'm used to it. I pick them off my hound dog all the time and she never says thank you." He was out the door now ready to leave. Then he leaned back through the door for a moment and said with a grin, "She does lick my hand though!" The screen door slammed.

Latina's face was burning as she whirled about and hurried into the house. The blue pickup laughed its rattle all the way back down the driveway.

Latina leaned against the rusty bridge railing and absently dribbled tiny pebbles through her fingers to the stream below. A swift bubbling current disguised the effects of the falling pebbles as though they'd never been dropped.

If only it were that easy to erase the harsh words she'd exchanged with her mother a few moments earlier. But the words, and the slamming of the front door as she ran out, still echoed in her ears.

It was Friday, and throughout the long, boring week her father had spent contented hours in his study and Dirk incessantly roamed about the woods in search of new discoveries. The men of the family were already deliriously happy with the summer arrangements, and her mother was becoming more so each day.

Yesterday her mother had purchased several potted plants at a roadside stand and this morning she had set about to replant them in hanging planters. When she asked Latina to lend a hand it was the last straw.

"What an absolute gas!" she said. "Spending my summer playing around with dirt and potted plants."

In a controlled voice her mother remarked that Latina could find something to keep her occupied if she tried.

"I'd have to try all right," came Latina's bitter reply. "For the crime of being an active, fun-loving teenager, I've been banished into exile in this backwoods, no-man's land, and now my punishment is to find something to do here."

She'd then fled from the house, charging up the road in a direction she'd never yet been. How could her parents be so unfeeling? Of course, she loved t hem. Among all her friends, she felt she had the best parents of all. And even now she wanted to please them, but visions of the cove tormented her as she compared it to this place.

And then there was Tully Clouse. His appearance at the house last evening to help her father dig postholes sent her scurrying to her room. After he and her father had worked a while in the cool, lavender evening, she heard him playing on his harmonica. The tunes that floated up into her partially opened window had irritated her as much as his laughing eyes. When she went over to close the window, she thought he glanced up at her from where he was perched on the tailgate of his old blue pickup. She stayed away from the window after that.

He lived up this road somewhere. She knew because every day his pickup rumbled by in a cloud of dust from this direction. It wouldn't have surprised Latina if this dusty little road simply wound around up the hill and disappeared into the side of the mountain. It was that kind of country. Strange—with strange people inhabiting it.

Still leaning over the bridge, staring down at the stream, Latina noticed sunlight reflecting off a metallic object and wondered what it was. She looked for a way down to the streambed. At the far end of the bridge, she found a slightly obscured pathway through the underbrush that led down to the water's edge. The stream was narrow with pebbled banks spreading out on either side.

Precariously, she made her way down the path only to discover the object wasn't metal at all, but a small rock glittering in the light that filtered through the dense trees. She stuffed it in her jeans pocket to give to Dirk later.

Picking her way cautiously along the stream, she looked for other interesting rocks for her brother. Presently, the water widened into a faster current. She pulled off her tennis shoes and waded ankle-deep. Each step in the cold water made her catch her breath. This clear water no doubt came from the underground caves her father had told her about. Glancing behind her she could see nothing but the stream and trees.

A series of gentle falls forced her to step out of the water and onto the bank. She put her shoes back on and made her way easily through the trees, up the incline and then back toward the water again. But at this point, it was no longer a small stream. Before her lay a mirrored pool of azure water surrounded by willows. Directly across the pool, rising up out of the undergrowth and half smothered by ivy, was a deserted gristmill. Its mammoth waterwheel, still intact, was poised above its wavering image reflected in the still water.

To the right of where she stood was a vast stone over-hang. Moving toward it, she sat down on the flat rocks beneath. It was like a cave. She could sit under the overhang and not touch her head on the damp rocks above.

As she surveyed the scene, suddenly the desire welled up within her to capture it on canvas. What a challenge that would be. The few paintings she'd done in the past were admired by her parents. They had encouraged her to pursue her talent, but there was never a moment to spare. Last summer, her mother had even purchased art supplies and canvases, but Latina laid them aside, ignoring the craggy cliffs at Periwinkle that begged to be painted.

Kent would love this place, she told herself smiling. Just as they had loved the ocean together. If he should decide to come miles out of his way to see her, now she would have something special to share with him. They would come here and spend the afternoons together.

But did he care enough to come? He'd cared enough to write last winter—surely that proved something. She dared not admit to herself that there weren't nearly as many letters to her as she had mailed to him.

A rustle on the rocky ledge above startled her from her thoughts. She froze as a small greenish-brown lizard slithered down the rock surface toward her. It stopped close to her, blinking like a tiny prehistoric monster. She reached for a rock to throw and her movement sent him gliding away.

For all its beauty, this wasn't a very safe place to be. Distressing thoughts of rattlesnakes haunted her as she set out for home. A sense of relief flooded over her once she reached the safety of the road.

CHAPTER FOUR

The car windows were rolled down and the fragrant breeze blew in on her face and hair. Latina usually despised having her hair windblown, but when driving with Donna Dee, for some reason it didn't seem to matter.

Her new friend was discussing her secretarial position at the Palatka law firm. "No one was more shocked than me when I landed this job. Kids in our consolidated high school look down on us kids from Zell's Bush as if we aren't quite up to snuff. But when I was at business school, I studied extra hard to prove them wrong—and I did it!" Her short dark curls bobbed as she spoke. "I know a proudful look isn't becoming, but when my old school chums walk past the office and there I am at the front desk of Jenner, Jenner and Sons, I feel like the tall hog at the trough"

Latina laughed at her new friend's way of talking. She wished she could relate to that feeling of accomplishment, but she could think of very few things in her life of which she could be justifiably proud. It was a disturbing thought.

Donna Dee parked the car near Palatka's massive stone courthouse and they strolled across the square to Larsen's Drug Store. They sat in a front booth near the windows in full view of the oak-shaded courthouse square.

"It's my shorthand I'm struggling with," Donna Dee admitted, back again on the subject of her job. "I still get skitterish when those nice lawyers start dictating important letters to me. I know I could do better."

"What you need is someone to dictate practice letters to you," Latina suggested. "There's a typing workbook in the bookcase at the house that is filled with all types of business letters. How would it be if we got together some evening and I dictated to you?"

"Oh would you mind, Latina? I know it would help so much. It's right nice of you to offer."

They ordered Cokes and Donna Dee introduced Latina to the waitress and to several other young people seated in adjoining booths. Their easy conversation and good-natured ribbing could easily have come from Wally's Grill near her school in Eagleton. Or for that matter, like the drugstore at Periwinkle Cove where she and Kent first met.

Returning to their own conversation, Donna Dee said with a knowing smile, "I bet you didn't spend your evenings back home dictating business letters."

Latina wanted to say, "You're right. Especially in the summer." But she pushed those thoughts aside. "No matter, I'd love to help you. Besides, I might have to take shorthand myself next year. Mother says it'll help in taking notes at college."

"You're going to college?"

"Both my parents teach at our local college." Latina stirred the ice in her cup with her straw. "I suppose I'd be a family disgrace if I didn't go."

Donna Dee's green eyes were wide. "You're so blessed. What will you study?"

Latina stared out the window for a moment. Her mother often asked the same question. "Plan your high school subjects to fit in with your major," she'd say. But for the life of her, Latina had no idea what her life goals were.

She chose to evade the question altogether with a quick, "I'm not sure yet," then changed the subject. "Is there an art store in this town? I'd like to buy paints and canvases and try my hand at a scene I saw yesterday."

Her friend nodded. "The Hobby House. Just down the street from the law office. Scads of tourists come through here who need art supplies. They're attracted to our scenic hills. So you're an artist?"

"I've dabbled at it," she answered carefully. "My folks think I have talent, but you know how parents are."

Later, at the Hobby House, Latina not only found her supplies, but also a wooden carrying case in which she could cart everything to the millpond. They also stopped at the hardware store where she purchased three packages of batteries for the transistor radio. If she were in for the duration, she might just as well gear up for survival.

On the way back to the car, Donna Dee took her by the office where she worked. Since it was Saturday the office was closed, but they peered in the window through cupped hands like children at a toy shop. At that moment, a voice sounded from behind them.

"Shopping?"

As they whirled about Donna Dee nearly stumbled over Latina's wooden case at her feet. "Oh Mr. Jenner," she gasped. "I didn't think anyone'd be anywhere near the office on Saturday."

The casually dressed young man was visibly amused as his secretary regained her composure. When she had caught her breath, she introduced Latina to the youngest members of the family law firm, Brad Jenner.

"Welcome to the Ozarks, Miss Harmen," Brad said, giving her a firm handshake. "I see you're planning to take some of our fair land home with you." He indicated the paint case which she'd now picked up and was holding.

"I'm attempting to anyway," she said with a polite smile.

"Well, we must be on our way," Donna Dee said as she tugged on Latina's arm. "See you Monday."

Later, when they neared the Zell's Bush turnoff, Latina was surprised to find the trip home was so brief—unlike the endless drive the day they'd arrived. The two girls had talked nonstop the entire way.

"So what was it you found to paint?" Donna Dee asked as they crossed the rattling bridges past the sawmill.

"I went for a walk yesterday along a stream and came upon an old millpond. I'm going to try my hand with that."

"The old mill? Well, I never." She sounded surprised. "What is it?"

"I never would have guessed you'd get that far off the road."

Latina swallowed hard over this referral to her citified ways.

"Oh, I'm sorry, Latina," Donna Dee said quickly. "I didn't mean to be rude. I'm glad you discovered the millpond. It's such a pretty place. Before I started working, I used to go there myself and just sit. I'll be happy to see your pictures when you're finished."

As they were unloading Latina's purchases at the house, Donna Dee added as an afterthought, "I think you ought to know, Latina, that Collier Hunsecker sometimes sets traps in the valley down from the millpond. He's bent on trapping year-round even though it's against the law. Just keep your eyes open when you're in the brush. They're pretty easy to spot."

"If it's against the law, why doesn't someone turn him in?"

"Collier? Oh, honey, Zell's Bush is used to Collier. We just put up with him. He's got a mad on all the time. If someone turned him in and he got caught, he'd just have more to be mad about. He's awful bullheaded, that Collier is."

Latina was irritated. Now there was yet another fear to overcome if she were to return to her rendezvous spot and record it on canvas; steel traps set beneath the damp layers of rotting leaves on the forest floor. She wondered if the risk was worth it.

❧⟨◉⟩❧

The screams of the big saws pierced the night air as Latina turned into the drive of Garwood's Sawmill. This was the night she and Donna Dee set aside to work together. Latina had thought that surely by this time the men would have finished and gone home. She lifted her hair off her collar wishing she'd tied it up off her neck. The days were beginning to get sticky.

Grabbing the typing book from the seat beside her she walked quickly across the graveled area toward the house. Under one of the sheds, only Tully, Collier and one other man were working at the saws. They must be finishing up some special work, she thought. She'd hurry on before they saw her.

Tully was feeding a large plank of lumber through the saw to make what looked to be a small cut. Latina was at the point where the hard-packed dirt path split to go toward the sheds or toward the house, when out of the corner of her eye, she noticed Collier moving up behind Tully. Purposely, the boy knocked against the smooth plank of precision-cut lumber causing the saw to scream and tear jaggedly into the wood.

Latina stopped dead still. Mr. Garwood appeared out of nowhere, his face livid.

"That's gonna cost you, Clouse. That's not a nail file you're working with."

Collier had slipped away and was nonchalantly looking over a pile of scraps nearby. Latina regarded the scene with disgust. Mr. Garwood needed to know the truth. Abruptly she turned in their direction as Tully was calmly and respectfully apologizing.

"My fault, sir," he said. "It slipped. I won't let it happen again."

"You can bet on that. Another expensive slip like that and I'll see to it you won't have a chance to do it again."

Mr. Garwood's back was toward her. As he leaned over to inspect the cut, Tully happened to glance up and see her. Without a word, his clear eyes signaled to her not to interfere.

She hesitated, puzzled. It wasn't right to let Collier get away with such a malicious act. She pressed her lips together and slowed her steps. She needn't bow to Tully's wishes. She could certainly tell Mr. Garwood anything she pleased.

Collier turned from the scrap pile. Spying her, he said loudly, "My, my. Here's our quick-blooming Latina-Flower."

Mr. Garwood turned to look at her. "Evening, Miss Harmen. Donna Dee's up at the house," he said as if to let her know she had no business in the sheds.

She groped for words. "My father wanted me to be sure to remind Tully we'll need him to help out up at our place tomorrow when he's off work," she said awkwardly. Her eyes went from Mr. Garwood's lined face to Tully's young one.

"Thanks," Tully said, his eyes meeting hers.

Deliberately, Latina forced her legs into measured steps up the winding path, resisting the urge to run. Well, she told herself, that should teach her something about butting into other people's affairs. Whether Tully was afraid of his weird cousin, or even threatened by him, it was none of her business. She was quite breathless as she approached the Garwood's front door.

Etta Ann met her with a hug and led her to where Donna Dee was waiting. She stepped into a living room dominated by a squat, black wood-burning heating stove—cool and unused in the summer's warmth. The wallpaper, the linoleum, the braided rug, even the couch- and chair-throws were of many colors and patterns, seemingly purchased, or acquired, for service only. Nothing matched. However, there was an unmistakable warmth that appealed to Latina. She felt instantly at home.

The two girls spread out their books and papers on the dining room table, and Latina began dictating letter after letter. By the end of the evening, Donna Dee was whipping out the swirled characters as fast as Latina could dictate.

"I don't think it's the shorthand that's the problem, Donna Dee," Latina teased. "Perhaps it's the effect of a handsome young attorney who does the dictating."

"It's more like the effect of his daddy," Donna Dee defended herself quickly. "That man can be as ornery as an old setting hen."

Before Latina left, Etta Ann offered them a snack of warm cornbread and syrup. Latina tried to imagine her reaction if her mother had offered her friends a snack of cornbread. With a twinge of shame, she had to admit she would have been mortified.

Several days later, Latina packed her paints and walked to the millpond. Her parents had announced they were going to a nearby lake to fish for the afternoon. Dirk immediately began noisily sorting through his tackle box out on the back porch.

"I think I'll stay behind," Latina told them. Noticing her mother's look of disappointment, she added, "I hate to fish, and I thought I'd bet started on some painting today."

Upon hearing the word *painting*, the disappointment seemed to fade. "Suit yourself," her mother said, "but just remember, we may not be back till after dark."

Due to recent night rains, the little hill stream had swollen since Latina's first visit. The day was warm and steamy heat rose from the damp earth giving off a rich, earthy smell. There were fewer places to walk in the pebbled stream now. Empty-handed she could have waded, but the case made it awkward, so she walked along the bank though thick branches that lashed her cheeks and briars that prickled through her jeans.

When she thought of Collier's steel traps, she wanted to turn and run, but the gurgling of the waterfalls told her the mill was near.

Balancing her art case, she made her way through the trees to the smooth rock precipice beneath the jutting rock overhang. Everything was just as it had been the day she'd discovered it—just as beautiful; just as serene. Spreading out an old blanket she'd brought along, she settled down with sketchbooks and pencils.

"It's simply too exquisite," she whispered. Could she ever capture the veil of mist that hung in the air near the overhang? "A false start is better than no start at all," her father used to tell her. Well, she would start!

The air was heavy and warm, even in the shady recesses of the overhang. Drops of perspiration trickled beneath her light cotton blouse, but she hardly noticed. She'd planned to stop and eat the sandwich she'd packed, but found herself holding the sandwich with her left hand while continuing to place finishing touches here and there on the sketches.

She hadn't noticed the tops of the trees stirring with the first moving of the cooler air that had arrived to clash head-on with the pocket of muggy, warmer air. Not having been reared in these hills, she was ignorant of the significance of these events. Up until now she'd experienced only the gentle rains, not a full-flung violent storm.

Enclosed in the thick woods and sheltered beneath the overhang, she was unable to see the thick boiling clouds moving in. By the time she felt the first rush of cooler air, fat raindrops were plopping into the water.

"No matter," she assured herself. "A little rainstorm—I can easily wait out a little rainstorm."

Stubbornly, she continued to sketch, confident it would soon cease. But it did not cease, nor did it let up once the torrents began to fall. She smoothed ringlets away from her face and peered up through the trees. Then she gathered her supplies into the case. "It'll surely be over in a minute. There's no sense in getting soaked. I can wait."

The hills echoed with violent groaning winds as a bolt of lightning pierced the sky followed by a crash of thunder.

Latina drew the old blanket around her shoulders and cowered beneath the ledge. She couldn't bear to think that she might be trapped her all night. She placed her art case far back where the rock formations met in a crevice. Better for it to be left behind than to be ruined as she returned home.

The water was steadily rising. Now it was swiftly rushing over the lower part of the ledge where she had been sitting. Quickly she pulled the blanket tightly around her and rushed out into the storm, hoping she could make it to the road safely.

She fought against the branches and tangling vines. The driving rain made any progress, even a few feet, a vain struggle. She'd intended to follow the streambed, but the stream wasn't in its bed. After stepping calf-deep in the overflow, she was forced to follow at a distance.

After what seemed to be an eternity of fighting, Latina sensed the undergrowth was thinning into a clearing. Surely this was the road. Now it would be a simple matter to run down the muddy track toward home. Her parents would be worried by this time.

She stared in disbelief through the silver sheets of rain at the mill on the opposite bank. She had walked in a complete circle. Her fears had become reality—the hills truly had swallowed her!

It was because of the roar of the storm that she ignored the first calls of her name. It was impossible. She was dreaming; no one knew she was here. She heard it from across the rushing water of the stream. She strained her eyes to make out the form.

It looked like...but it couldn't be. Tully!

CHAPTER FIVE

Tully was calling and waving his arms over his head on the far bank of the rushing stream. "The rocks!" she could hear him calling. "Below the bend. Cross there!"

Cross? Why? All she wanted was to get to the road and then on home. It was growing darker every minute. She plunged on forward.

She caught glimpses of Tully's red plaid shirt moving through the trees as he ran on ahead. When she reached the bend where the large boulders protruded up from the water, he was there calling for her to cross over. She pulled the soaked blanket tighter around her shoulders. There was no way she could make herself cross. And besides that was the wrong way.

She'd not taken ten more steps when she felt his hands firm on her shoulders. How had he crossed so quickly?

"Latina," he shouted, straining to make himself heard over the deluge. "My house is just the other side of that ridge." He waved a hand in the direction from which he'd come. "I'll help you cross. You can rest and get dry there."

Latina pulled away and stumbled backward. "I've got to get home. My parents don't know where I am. Please just get me to the road. Please!"

He reached for her arm, but she pulled back again.

"Listen to me! It's three times as far to your place as mine. There could be flash flooding at the bridges. You might not even make it to the road."

He stepped toward her. Grabbing the edges of the blanket, he secured it around her, then swept her up in his arms pressing her against him. "I can't just leave you out here in this mess." As she struggled to get loose, he said, "You'd better quit that mule-kicking, or you'll land us both in the creek."

Latina couldn't bear to look as he plunged across, making his way partly on the rocks, partly in the rising water with her in his arms. She buried her face in his wet shirt. Safely on the opposite bank, he strode with her still in his arms, over the hill, across a gully and halfway up the next hill to his house.

"We're almost there," he told her.

His boots made a thudding noise as he tramped up the wooden steps. He threw the door open and set Latina down.

Kneeling in front of a wood-burning heating stove was a diminutive lady dressed in faded jeans and a boyish-looking flannel shirt. "Land sakes, Tully," she said jumping up from where she'd been stoking the fire. "A body never knows what you'll be carrying home next, do they?"

"Mama," Tully said. "This here's Latina Harmen. Her family's staying at the Nettleton place for the summer."

"The folks you been working for? Well, well. Pleased to meet you child. I'm Jayleen. Got caught in a bad one, didn't you?" She stepped toward Latina and surprised her with an unrestrained hug. "We'll get you out of these wet things."

Latina was painfully aware of the growing puddle of rainwater spreading at her feet on the blue-flowered linoleum.

Jayleen stepped back and sized up her guest. "I think I have some britches and a shirt that'll fit you." Then she added, "Althea's asleep on my bed, so you'll have to change in Tully's room. Come on now before you catch your death."

"My folks," Latina said, the concern still foremost in her mind.

"Sorry, dear, but we don't have a telephone. But perhaps Tully can drive down to check the bridges later. I doubt if you can cross tonight." Jayleen ushered her through a small living room and into Tully's bedroom.

Within minutes, Latina had changed into the dry jeans and shirt both of which were worn and faded but clean and dry.

She rubbed at her matted hair with the towel Jayleen had given her and studied the room with interest. A rustic set of bookshelves were filled with volumes of poetry, a number of the classics, and Sandburg's complete works of *Lincoln*. Beneath the shelves, an unsteady card table provided a makeshift desk.

Lying face down and open on the table was a book of poetry. Latina picked it up and saw it was open to Tennyson's "Flower in the Crannied Wall." She remembered studying the poem in her literature class back home. She scanned the short verse.

Flower in the crannied wall,
I pluck you out of the crannies,
I hold you here, root and all, in my hand,
Little flower -but if I could understand
What you are, root and all, and all in all,
I should know what God and man is.

In Latina's mind she couldn't connect the long-legged boy propped back in a chair at Boles' Grocery with a young man living in a bedroom like this. Each item in the room was in place, unlike Dirk's disaster at home. She had assumed all guys lived in utter confusion, stuffing half their belongings under the bed.

On a whatnot shelf above the bed were several wooden carvings like the ones she'd seen at the sawmill. She picked up a little squirrel, turning it over in her hands.

A knock at the door prompted her to replace the figurine on the shelf. "Dinner's ready, Latina." It was Jayleen's voice.

"I'm coming. Thank you." She wrapped her wet things in the blanket and walked out into the kitchen. Tully was seated by the stove.

She smiled sheepishly. "You can have your room now. Sorry I took so long." She paused. "And I'm sorry I gave you such a bad time out there." She was uncomfortably aware of her bedraggled appearance.

"Don't give it another thought." Tully grinned at her and headed to his room to change.

"That old storm take you by surprise?" Jayleen asked.

"Yes, ma'am. I've never seen a storm come that fast, and I was so far from home. I tried to wait it out, but when the water began to rise, I panicked."

"I've lived around her all my life, but I still get jumpy when a storm starts a-brewing."

Tully then appeared in dry clothes. "Want me to wake Althea?" he asked his mother as he effortlessly lifted the heavy pot of stew from her hands and placed it on the table.

"Please do, Tully. She can eat with us and get to know Latina."

He disappeared into the only other bedroom in the small house and returned with a thin little girl in his arms. Her head was cocked like a fragile bird's.

Latina was astonished. The figurine at the sawmill—it had been carved in the likeness of this little girl. The small-boned child labored to lift her head and focus her eyes to see this stranger.

On one other occasion in her life, Latina had been around a child with just such an affliction. Her Scout troop had visited a learning center for handicapped children when she was in grade school. Although the other girls were repulsed, Latina had been drawn by an unspeakable compassion that she'd expressed to no one else.

"Althea." Tully's voice was soft and gentle. "This is Latina. She's come to visit us."

"Hi, Althea." Latina said, "I'm very pleased to meet you."

In the silence that followed, the wood stove gave off its friendly popping noises. Then Althea strained to lift her head straight. "Ah-teen-ah," she pronounced slowly.

Jayleen applauded. "Wonderful Althea. You did great."

Tully set her down on a chair where Jayleen firmly tied her in with a dish towel. Latina could see there was no other way the child could remain upright. Jayleen and Tully took turns helping her eat.

After supper, Tully excused himself to go out and "check on the animals." After he was gone, Latina asked Jayleen about the books in his room.

"Isn't that just a sight?" Jayleen said with pride in her voice. "That other professor, the one who was here last year, took a liking to Tully and gave him several. Other's he's just collected along the way. I guess since he loves them so much, he has a way of finding them. In old flea markets and the like."

Latina took a towel from a towel rack and wiped the dishes as Jayleen washed. No dishwasher in this home.

"Where does Tully attend school?"

"He doesn't. At least now he doesn't." Jayleen let her soapy hands hang limp over the sink for a moment. "He was tops in his junior class at the valley consolidated school, but that was the year we learned we could get a tutor for Althea. He quit school to work at the mill full-time to provide the money for the tutor." She plunged her hands back into the water and brought up a chipped plate to wash. "Since his daddy died, Tully's really stepped in to take over.

"Well-meaning folks told us to put Althea in a home somewhere. Then I could get a job and Tully could finish his schooling. But Tully was dead set on keeping Althea right here. 'Can't nobody love her like we can,' he says to me. I agreed of course, but it broke my heart when he quit school."

Jayleen wrung out her dish cloth and began to wipe down the small counter area. "He would have graduated last month when he turned eighteen. All his life he's dreamed of graduating from college, but now that dream just keeps fading away."

Latina could see it was a dead-end street for Tully to continue at the sawmill. It was a sure bet he had no future there.

When Tully returned he found Latina on the floor playing with Althea. He flashed her a smile of appreciation. "I took a run down to the bridge," he told them as he hung his black rain slicker on a hook near the back door. "There's flash flooding in the valley. Can't hardly see the first bridge at all."

Jayleen looked up from the jeans in her lap that she was mending. "Guess everyone's safe on high ground. At least I hope so."

"No way you can get home tonight, Latina," Tully told her. "I'll just bed down in front of the stove and you can have my room."

"Oh no, really," she protested. "I couldn't take your room. I can easily sleep here on the couch. I'll be fine."

Tully's eyes twinkled and she wondered if he was laughing at her again. "The couch it is," he said.

It was a surprise to Latina that as she settled under the soft quilts, she felt wrapped in a peace that she hadn't felt since leaving her own room in Eagleton.

❧◈❧

The next morning after they finished a hearty breakfast of ham and biscuits, Tully invited her to help him feed the *livestock*.

"Would Althea like to come?"

The little girl picked up on it immediately. She was excited to go see the "chi-chi's," which Latina was informed meant chickens.

It was apparent that Tully and Jayleen had invested time to teach this girl to be as independent as possible. Althea walked with a rolling gait, with her head cocked, but her infectious joy bubbled forth continuously.

Latina held her hand and helped her down the porch steps as Tully led the way across the wet yard and past a large washtub filled with new petunia plants. A liver-colored coon hound moseyed toward them, her tail beating out an excited welcome.

"This the hound dog with the ticks?" Latina and Althea both patted the dog's head.

"That's her. Latina, meet Rosie. Rosie, Latina."

Rosie then politely sat at Latina's feet and offered a wet paw, which Latina shook. "My, such manners."

"It's the environment. High class place we got here."

Latina blushed. Had he guessed her initial thoughts upon arriving at Zell's Bush?

After feeding the flock of cackling chickens, he took her into a small wooden building filled with cages. Within the cages were squirrels, raccoons, rabbits and one badger—some with splints on their legs.

"What's this? You own zoo?" she asked.

"Sort of a way station," he explained as he refilled water dishes in each cage. "I help them until they can help themselves again."

Althea wiggled her fingers in a rabbit's cage and giggled as she touched the fur.

"These must be victims of your cousin's illegal trapping activities."

"How'd you know about Collier?"

"Donna Dee. She warned me to look out for the traps, just in case."

"That's what I was doing before the storm hit—checking the traps. I saw you with your sketchbook at the millpond, so after the storm hit I thought I better go back and check on you." Then he added, "Because of the high water *and* the submerged traps."

She felt her face coloring. She'd been watched without even realizing it. A spooky feeling, but at the same time, she was eternally grateful.

"And by the way," he went on, "I'm obliged to you for keeping quiet when Collier knocked the plank into the saw the other night."

"Don't mention it. If you want to let him get away with murder, it's none of my concern." Every time she thought about Collier, she got angry. "Is he responsible for all this damage?" she asked with a sweep of her hand.

He nodded. "I find them in the traps. If they're still alive I nurse them back to health and let them go again."

Latina wanted to make a snappy comeback, but thought better of it. "Dirk would love this place," she said instead. "He's crazy about animals."

"Is he? Then you'll have to bring him for a visit some-time."

"I'll do that."

❧◉❧

By late afternoon, the waters had receded enough for Tully and Latina to cross the bridge and drive to her house. Her family had just arrived and had no idea she'd been gone the entire night. They too had been unable to get home and had spent the night at the Boles'.

"Seems to me we'd better have a phone installed," her father said at supper that evening. "The lack of communication around this community is gosh awful. Especially when you're cut off on all sides by rushing water."

Latina was jubilant. Now she could give the number to Kent when she wrote again. If the flood was to blame, then she was thankful even for the flood.

"Did you know," she said changing the subject, "that Tully has a handicapped younger sister?"

She went on to describe Althea's condition and how Jayleen and Tully had diligently taught her, and how Tully had quit school to work and provide funds for a tutor.

"Has he ever thought about taking correspondence courses?" her mother asked, her professional instinct piqued.

"I don't know. At least the subject never came up."

Why hadn't she thought of that, Latina wondered. It seemed to be the perfect answer. But what if there wasn't enough money even for that? And how could she suggest it? He might resent her as an interfering busybody.

"I could help him get started," her mother went on. "I wonder what kind of student he is."

"Tops in his junior class, Jayleen told me."

"Ah," was all her mother said.

CHAPTER SIX

Latina carefully picked her way along the streambed, now so placid after the turmoil of the past week. When she reached the millpond, she found to her delight that, just as she had hoped, her paints were still safe and dry deep within the rock crevice. She sat down and was soon lost in her work.

By late afternoon, she was at last ready to leave. She'd just emerged from the underbrush and was climbing up the bank to the bridge when she saw the old blue pickup rattle by with Tully at the wheel and Donna Dee beside him. Odd, but she'd never thought of them as a couple. But it certainly made sense. After all, they'd know one another for years. She pushed that thought out of her mind and continued her walk homeward.

She arrived at the house to find a letter waiting on the kitchen table. It made her forget about Tully, Donna Dee, and everything else that had to do with Zell's Bush. She tore it open and read:

Dear Latina:

Mexico is a blast! I'll be flying into Springfield on Saturday and will rent wheels. Send me a map so I can find my way to the majestic city of Zell's Bush.

And he signed it, *Love, Kent.* She rubbed her finger over the word *love.* Kent was coming! She could hardly believe it. She pushed the letter into her pocket and went outside so she'd meet her parents as soon as they returned from their fishing excursion and give them the news.

Her parents had never really accepted Kent. Not that they'd ever said anything unkind. On the contrary, they were almost too nice, but she could tell how they really felt.

Dirk had never been subtle about expressing his feelings. "Yuck," he said, screwing up his face in disgust when he heard the news of Kent's upcoming visit. "Just when we were beginning to have fun, that snob has to come and remind us how the other half lives." Her parents made vague comments such as, "That's nice, dear." She had no one with whom she could share her joy and excitement.

Later that evening, Latina sat by her bedroom window composing her reply to Kent. Below her, she could hear Tully and her father laughing and talking as they worked together mending the fence in the side yard. They seemed to enjoy one another's company.

When she'd finished the brief note, she sketched out a map and placed the two sheets in an airmail envelope to be mailed out the following morning. Then decided to go down and talk to Tully about taking correspondence courses, assuming her dad hadn't already mentioned it.

She found him sitting on the tailgate of his pickup. The melody from his harmonica had reached her before she came around the corner of the house. He caught sight of her and stopped in the middle of the tune, lowering the harmonica to give her a slow smile.

She hesitated, then stepped to the side of the truck, resting her arms on the cool metal. "Where is everyone?" she asked.

Tully slipped the harmonica into his shirt pocket. "Dirk's out catching lighting bugs, and your daddy went in to get us some lemonade."

"Dirk's got enough fireflies now to light up the entire house. Mom and I keep letting them go again. Dirk loves this place."

"And you're still not sure." He was studying her face. Then he said, "Flower in the crannied wall..." He stopped and swung his legs up into the pickup bed to sit more comfortably. "I pluck you out of the crannies, I hold you here, root and all, in my hand little flower..." His hands were cupped as though he were holding the flower of which he spoke. Now he looked at her with that maddening twinkle in his eyes.

She felt her face redden. "How did you know I looked?"

"You left the book face up. I had it face down. I'm an awful stickler for details."

"You have a terrific library," she said in an attempt to mask her discomfort.

"Glad you like it. Feel free to come and check it out anytime. And just so you know, Althea is still talking about you."

"She's a precious little girl. You and your mother have done wonders with her."

"Not everyone agrees with you, sorry to say. Most of the time she cringes around strangers." Tully gazed past her now, staring out into the darkness. Latina waited, having nothing to say and not wanting to say the wrong thing. "Few people around here warm up to her the way you did. They make thoughtless remarks. This may sound strange, but she knows the difference."

Bringing his attention back to the present, he said, "Say, you left a couple of hair-bobs on my dresser."

"My barrettes? I'd forgotten all about them."

"Althea found them. She pitched a little fit until Mama put them in her hair. She points to them and tries to say your name."

"Really?"

"How about you and Dirk going with Althea and me on a picnic up at the millpond on Saturday? The two of you would be great for Althea—she needs to be around people more."

Latina was within a breath of agreeing when she suddenly remembered about Ken. "I'd love to, Tully, but I have a friend coming from Mexico on his way back to the East Coast. I don't know how long he'll be staying."

"Some other time, maybe."

"Sure. Some other time." In the silence that followed, Latina decided she'd ask what had been on her mind.

"May I ask a question that may be none of my business?"

"Shoot."

"Why didn't your high school counselors help you finish up your senior year so you could graduate on time?

Tully pulled the harmonica back out of his pocket and rubbed it on his sleeve. "You have to understand, Latina. No one expects a guy from Zell's Bush to graduate. Most of them quit for one reason or another. I was no different to them."

"But you *are!*" she interjected too quickly. "I mean, you only quit because you had to."

"They don't know the difference."

"Did you ever consider taking correspondence courses? Mom and Dad could help you choose the ones you need and show you how to fill out the forms and all. Mom knows all about where to send off for them and everything." She stopped. She was talking too fast.

He sat quietly studying the small instrument in his hand. Had someone taught him to play, she wondered, or was it as natural to him as creating beauty by carving out scraps of wood?

Presently his blue eyes held hers again. "I guess you could say I threw in the towel. It seemed like such a far-fetched dream to think I could ever make it to college. When I saw I'd have to work full-time to pay for Althea's teacher and take care of Mama too, I closed that door in my mind completely. Not too smart, huh?"

He vaulted out of the pickup suddenly and stood to his full height. "Correspondence courses." He spoke it slowly as though trying out the thought. "Like through the mail, right?"

She nodded.

"Latina-Flower," he said, "I believe that door in my mind is still a tad bit ajar. Let's go talk to the professors."

It was a nerve-wracking chore to prepare a room for some-one accustomed to the best, Latina thought as she put the finishing touches on the downstairs bedroom. The family hadn't needed the room and so they'd kept it closed off. She hoped Kent would appreciate the wild flowers she had carefully arranged in vases and placed on the dresser. But then he was coming from an exclusive Acapulco hotel where they probably put fresh flowers in his room every day.

Smoothing the quilt once more, she caught sight of her nails. What a mess! There'd been no reason to fix them until now. She'd manicure them tonight—in time for his arrival the next afternoon. Everything would be perfect. What would her living in a farmhouse matter if she looked just right for him? Surely he liked her for who she was and not for where she lived.

A knock at the front door startled her from her thoughts. "I'll get it," she called to her family who were all in the kitchen. She stepped quickly through the front room, retying her wraparound skirt as she went.

She flung open the heavy front door to find none other than Kent Starner standing there dressed smartly in dark navy slacks and a white blazer.

"Surprise!" he practically shouted, flashing his wonderful smile.

Everything in her wanted to slam the door. She had carefully planned every detail to look perfect for the moment of his arrival. Surely, this couldn't be happening to her.

"Kent," she said helplessly, her hand flying to the bandana that held back her unwashed hair. Stray wisps floated from beneath it. "I thought you said tomorrow." She forced a weak smile.

"Some greeting—after my coming all this way. Aren't you going to even ask me in?" He bent down to pick up the two pieces of matching olive-green luggage at his feet. "I'm ready for my glimpse of authentic rural Americana. Even though I got quite a dose just now coming up those hills"

Awkwardly, she stepped back. "Sure. Sure, Kent. Come on in."

"A guy in our group unexpectedly decided to stay on an extra day," Kent explained, setting his luggage on the braided rug in the front room. Latina watched as he slowly took it all in. "This guy was looking for someone to switch out plane reservations, so I spoke up. Wanted to get here sooner to be with the most beautiful girl in the world," he added.

There it was. That charm that had won her over last summer at the cove. It would have been music to her ears had she felt even remotely beautiful at the moment.

Mercifully, her mother chose that very moment to break into the strained silence. "Who's here, Latina? Well, Kent! Hello there and welcome to Zell's Bush. You're looking dashing as usual."

Catching Latina's expression she added, "Weren't you due in tomorrow?"

"He caught an earlier flight," Latina answered for him.

"Well, no matter. We're glad to have you. Latina's been busy fixing up the downstairs bedroom. It's no Waldorf Astoria, but I'm sure you'll be comfortable. Since we're all upstairs, it'll be nice and private."

Kent laughed. "No bell hops, no room service, no penthouse suite. I'll try to make a go of it, Mrs. Harmen."

Just as Latina took a breath to say she'd show him the room, Tully and the professor came down the hall from the kitchen. She'd completely forgotten that Tully had been sitting at the kitchen table with her parents for the past hour sorting out the correspondence courses he should take.

As her father made casual introductions, Latina immediately sensed Kent's reaction to Tully. She twisted the ties of her wraparound skirt around her fingers. Tully's "Howdy" sounded so backwoodsy. Why couldn't he just say, "Hi there," the way normal people did?

"I was just leaving," Tully announced walking toward the front door. "Thank you, Professor and Mrs. Harmen for all your help and time. I'll head for the house now." To Kent, he added, "Hope you enjoy your stay with these fine folks."

For a breathless moment, Latina prayed Tully would exit without so much as a glance in her direction, but it was not to be. He paused to let his smiling eyes rest on her. She felt Kent looking at Tully and then at her. "Good-bye Latina-Flower," Tully said.

Anger welled up inside her. He had recognized her predicament and intentionally made it worse. She stood there paralyzed until Tully left, carefully closing the door behind him.

"As I was driving through all those hairpin curves," Kent commented dryly, "I felt sorry for you being stuck out here in the boonies all alone. But I guess you aren't quite as lonely as I thought—*Latina-Flower.*"

"Now see here, Starner," her father spoke up. "Tully Clouse does part-time work for me. He was here to see me, not Latina."

"Daddy, really!" she blurted out more loudly than she intended. "Kent, let me show you the room we fixed up for you." She gave her parents a withering look that she meant to dismiss them. Her mother gently ushered her husband back toward the kitchen, instructing Kent to let her know if he needed anything.

Once in the front bedroom, Kent placed the smaller suitcase on the bed and opened it. From beneath the closing, he brought out a small package and placed it in her hands. "For you."

"Thank you," Latina whispered. In the box lay a pair of delicate silver filigree earrings. Looking up at him, she added. "You did take us by surprise, you know. But I—I'm so glad you're here."

"Sweetheart, I tried to call from the airport in Springfield, but I couldn't get through. I didn't want to waste any more time, so I just came." He couldn't resist adding, "I guess I did kind of surprise you. Does King Kong spend much time around here?"

"A few evenings a week to help Dad. I never even notice when he's here." So Kent still found her attractive in spite of her old shoes, unkempt hair, and mangled nails. "I'll go change now and get all gussied up for you."

"Gussied up?" He gave a strained laugh. Not at all like the laugh she remembered. "Is that an Ozarkian term?" He reached out and placed his hands on her arms. "You look gussied up enough for me."

For days and weeks, she'd dreamed of falling into his arms, but now she found herself pulling away. "I'll change and then show you around this place," she said awkwardly, then turned and left the room.

CHAPTER SEVEN

The rental car was a new-smelling, late-model sedan with powder-blue velour upholstery. Latina slid comfortably into the luxurious interior, feeling like royalty. What would it be like, she wondered, to date Kent on a steady basis? For the millionth time she wished they lived nearer one another. Why did they have to meet on a beach hundreds of miles from either of their homes?

After Kent's arrival she'd managed to get in a quick shower and shampoo, but the nails were a lost cause. Kent was in the kitchen talking to her mother when she appeared cleaned up and in a better frame of mind. Immediately he wanted to know what they should with the rest of the afternoon. That's when Latina suggested they go meet Donna Dee. As they drove down the winding hills to the sawmill, Latina tried to explain to Kent her feelings about the millpond.

"A pond with a deserted mill," he said. "Hm. Sounds okay, I guess, if that's what pushes your buttons. Say, sweetheart, did I tell you the color of the new sailboat? Sky blue! And it's a honey. Moves across the water like a dream. Wait'll you see what it can do." He reached over and took her hand as he maneuvered the car around curves and bridges with one hand on the wheel. "You *are* coming out to the coast for a week or two, aren't you?" he asked.

"To the coast?" She searched her mind. Had she said something—anything—to make him think...?

"I talked to Randy last week. He said Monique's there and all the gang. It's going to be a blast. We'll arrange it with Monique's folks for you to stay there."

"I don't know, Kent. My parents...."

"They'll understand. They don't expect you to stay out here in the sticks and fade into oblivion, do they?"

Latina's mother had never really approved of the fast-talking, presumptuous Monique, and quite truthfully, neither had she. At least not well enough to stay at her place for a week or more. But even if there were someone to stay with at the cove, her parents would never allow her to travel alone. And on top of all that, there simply wasn't enough money for such a trip. But how could someone like Kent understand a financial crunch?

"This is the turnoff," she told him.

Kent was forced to use both hands on the wheel to negotiate the rutted drive. "Give me a six-lane expressway any day," he muttered between clenched teeth as the car lurched about.

Latina tensed up at his irritation. His reference to the kids at the cove reminded her of all the things she was trying to forget—that there were beautiful people out there in the summer sun while she mildewed in the soggy backwoods.

"Whew, what a layout," he said as she led him up the path to the Garwood's front door. "This is Zell's Bush Industrial Park, right?"

"You guessed it." She laughed in an attempt to join in his banter.

Etta Ann was overjoyed to see Latina and meet her *feller*. Latina was relieved when Donna Dee came bouncing into the room. "Well, howdy folks. So this is Kent. Pleased to meet you."

"Howdy to you, too," Kent retorted, obviously amused by the greeting.

"You youngsters make yourselves right to home while I get some spiced cider poured up," Etta Ann said, smoothing her hands on her apron and heading for the kitchen.

Ken shook his head in disbelief, but Donna Dee was oblivious. She was chattering to Latina about the improvements in her shorthand. Some of her questions were aimed at Kent, who in return told her about his school in Boston and his recent graduation.

"So what does a person do about here for kicks?" Kent asked during a lull in the conversation. "I mean there must be some form of recreation somewhere."

"Oh sure!" Donna Dee nodded. "We don't just sit around picking our teeth on whittled splinters all day." Her easy joke brought a genuine laugh from Kent. "There's a nice beach and restaurant at Lake Lotawana about twenty-five miles from here."

"Lotawana? That name's for real?"

"It's an old Indian name," she explained. "The restaurant is built into the bluffs and overlooks the lake. The restaurant is all done up in a Hawaiian theme."

When she said Hawaiian it sounded like, Hi-wa-yan. Kent shot a grin at Latina that Donna Dee couldn't have missed.

"Now that sounds more our speed, doesn't it, Sweetheart," Kent said to Latina. To Donna Dee he said, "Hey, how about if you grab a guy and come along to make it a foursome tomorrow? We can swim in the afternoon and eat supper there in the evening. How about it?"

Donna Dee hesitated. "Sounds swell, but I don't know."

"Hey! Starner here will foot the bill." He jabbed a thumb at his chest. "No problem. Come on. How about it? It'll be fun. We'll be here to pick up you and your date just after lunch. You be ready, okay?"

Possibly only for Latina's sake, Donna Dee finally agreed.

There was no doubt in Latina's mind who Donna Dee's *date* would be, but there was no point telling Kent that now.

Latina awoke the next morning with a feeling of excitement. Her anxieties of the evening before had dissolved with the freshness of the morning. Today she'd be swimming with Kent just like last summer. From her dresser she pulled out her black swimsuit with the scarlet flower pattern and laid it out on the bed.

For the millionth time, she opened the small box holding her silver earrings. They were so stunning; so delicate. She dropped the box into her beach bag where she could retrieve them later and wear them for this special evening.

At that moment, her mother came to her bedroom door and surveyed the unmade bed and clothes strewn about the room.

"Oh Mom, help! What'll I wear this evening?"

She explained the day's plans and their decision to invite Donna Dee and her date. Her mother stepped to the closet and pulled out her lavender shirtwaist with the long sheer sleeves.

"This is wrinkle-resistant," she said. "Fold it into your beach bag and you'll look great. Comb your wet hair up on top your head and fasten your lavender flowers in the back."

It was a good idea, but Latina's mind was wandering to Tully Clouse.

Her mother stopped talking and looked at her. "You don't like the choice, or you're worried about something. Which?"

"Huh? Oh, no. I mean, yes. I agree with the lavender. It'll be fine, thanks." Why did her mother have to be so perceptive? "What's on the breakfast menu? Kent will probably be famished."

"Ham and pancakes sound okay?"

"Mm. Great. I'll be right down to help."

When she was alone again, she clutched the lavender dress and whirled about the room on giddy feet. How could she possibly be worried about this wonderful day? To think she would be spending it with the most dynamic, talented, handsome guy she'd ever known. And to think he'd come many miles out of his way just so see her!

But when she joined her mother in the kitchen, her mood had changed. Unbidden, memories of Tully came to her mind. Once again, she felt the power of his arms as he carried her through the storm, his determined blue eyes smiling encouragement at her.

"Latina, let's wait to see if everyone wants orange juice, shall we?"

Absently, Latina had been pouring juice into the tumblers. The juice glasses hadn't even been placed around yet.

"Sorry," she muttered.

Intermittently, Latina glanced at the door, anticipating Kent's entrance. She wondered nervously what it would be like to have him at a family meal.

"You're a bit flustered, Latina. Can't you calm down?"

She gave a silly grin and laughed. "I guess not."

Her father came through the kitchen door with a handful of notes that he placed beside his plate. His enthusiasm for the book was mounting daily.

"What're we waiting for?" he wanted to know.

Pauline took a glance out past the porch. "Well, Dirk's not here yet. I have no idea what he's up to so early."

Latina didn't know whether to wake Kent or not. He was no doubt tired after his trip.

The door to the porch slammed. "Let's eat," Dirk called out. "I'm starved." He loped to the kitchen sink to wash his hands with the dishwashing detergent. Working up a lather, he blew three king-sized bubbles through his fingers before rinsing. One floated over the pancakes and burst just before touchdown, sending a fine spray over the table.

"Where's Wonderboy?" he asked after he'd sat down. "Waiting for room service?" Ruthlessly he stabbed three pancakes.

"Still asleep," Latina explained coolly. "He was really tired."

"Yeah, I can imagine. Must be a tough drag to lounge around the beach at Acapulco. Took all his strength just to watch all those bikini beauties."

It was after eleven o'clock when Kent strolled through the house in his silk robe. Latina was on the back porch in a lawn chair reading.

"Hey, there you are," he called out from the kitchen. He strolled out and seated himself in the chair beside her. "Thanks for letting me sleep. I was beat. Say," he said, reaching out to touch her hair and letting his hand rest on her shoulder, "if this is being gussied up, I'm sorry I poked fun at the term. This color is great on you."

For one frozen moment, Latina thought he was going to lean over and kiss her. His hand moved to the back of her neck and he moved his face nearer hers.

With a slam of the door, Dirk exploded into the screened-in porch from outside. He spent hardly any time in the house—ever. "What's for lunch? I'm starved." Spotting, Kent, he added, "Well, whoop-de-doo! Up in time for lunch, Mr. Starner? Great move."

∙⟨◉⟩∙

Tully's pickup was parked by the sawmill when Latina and Kent pulled into the parking lot to pick up Donna Dee. The two of them were talking amiably as they came out of the Garwood's house, ignoring Kent who was revving the motor.

"Hill people don't move too fast, do they?" Kent said.

Latina caught the mood-change in his eyes as he realized he would be spending the day with Tully Clouse.

"Pleased to see you again, Starner," Tully said, helping Donna Dee into the back seat. "Thanks for the invitation. I haven't been for a swim at Lotawana for a coon's age."

"That long, huh?" Kent said, giving a quick glance in the rear view mirror. Gravel sprayed as he sped out of the drive and up the rutted road.

Donna Dee was puzzled. "You two met already?"

"Yesterday afternoon at my house," Latina explained. "Tully was talking to my dad when Kent arrived."

"Then you're already friends. That's super!"

Latina was painfully conscious of Donna Dee's pronunciation. Friends came out as "fra-yunds." She didn't dare look at Kent, but she could imagine his expression all too well.

"What do you do for excitement in this thriving metropolis?" Kent asked. "Watch them stock the grocery store?"

Latina tensed up, annoyed by the heavy sarcasm, but Donna Dee just laughed. "It may look boring to you, Kent," she said, "but you'd be surprised what a body can find to do when no one's around to provide the entertainment."

"I bet."

Donna Dee was right, Latina thought, her mind going to the hours she'd spent painting at the millpond. Lack of entertainment had forced her to discover her own resources.

"Sometimes," Tully's husky voice came directly behind her, "Orville and Maude Boles get into a fight with the feather dusters. That's dandy to watch."

Donna Dee giggled. "Oh, come on, Tully."

"Of course, Orville won't even get up to defend hisself. Just sits there and whacks at Maudie when she moves in too close." He gave each word an exaggerated drawl. "But she got him back the other day. Swept him clean off'n his chair."

Laughter bubbled up from Latina's midsection before she could think to contain it. Tully's quick wit amazed her.

Kent just scowled. He gazed straight ahead, occasionally breaking the silence to swear at a particularly sharp hairpin curve or a sudden bump in the road.

To Latina's surprise, Lake Lotawana was within an hour of Zell's Bush. They came upon it suddenly, nestled in the hills. The waters spread out before them azure and clear, with hardly a ripple disturbing the surface, sunlight sparkling all diamond-like. The lake appeared to go on for miles, bordered with tree-studded hills. Sailboats skimmed along in the distance and the intermittent hum of motor boats broke the silence.

Everyone piled out of the car to change in the little rundown bathhouses, after which they rushed down to the water's edge.

Kent took Latin by the hand to gently coax her in. Tully and Donna Dee had already dived in ahead of them and were swimming out toward deeper water where bright orange buoys marked the edge of the swim area.

The feel of Kent's hand, the look on his face, even the tone of his voice, swept her back to her memories of last summer at the cove. Now they could recapture those memories.

For a long time they just floated together in the water, too relaxed and lazy even to talk. Finally, by unspoken mutual consent, they swam to shallows and walked hand in hand to the warm rocks where they had left their towels.

"You know the millpond I told you about last evening?" Latina asked, shaking a miniature waterfall from her hair.

"The one with the deserted mill?" Kent asked, spreading his towel and lowering himself down on it.

"That's the one. Would you believe I've been painting the scene? It's quite a challenge. There's a mist over the water and a cave-like overhang. The light is pretty tricky..."

"That's a real shame, Sweetheart." Lying on his stomach now, Kent's voice was muffled into his arm.

"It's a what?" She must have heard him wrong.

He rolled over and looked at her. "Man it's a shame there's nothing more for you to do than to off all alone and paint. You'll get paranoid that way. Are you sure your folks won't let you stay with Monique for a week? They can't expect you to rot in this forsaken place just because your dad's a history nut."

Latina felt her shoulders stiffen. She'd been furious with her father for ruining her summer, but she admired his work intensely.

"I don't know, Kent. I really doubt they'll let me go."

He groaned then and turned back over to gaze out at the water. "This is nothing like Periwinkle Cove, huh."

She wanted to agree, but she also wanted to tell him that she thought the lake was beautiful in its own way. Couldn't there be room for both? Did one have to be better than the other? "But you'll soon be back where the waves are pounding," she said.

Far to her left, where the rocks and bluffs jutted out from a steep cliff-wall beneath where the restaurant was located, she saw Tully's form on the rocks. He stood their poised for a moment. Latina felt her breath catch as he leaped off executing a perfect dive into the water below.

"That's not for another week yet," Kent said, moving into a sitting position. He looked at her then out to the lake, then back at her. "You aren't trying to get rid of me, are you?" he asked accusingly.

She lay her head against his warm shoulder. "Never."

A fat candle anchored in a pink seashell flickered on their table—part of the Polynesian decor of the Kona Kai restaurant. Latina couldn't think of any place in Periwinkle Cove that was any more elegant. She stirred her juice cooler and wondered if Tully and Donna Dee were ill at ease. She hoped they wouldn't do or say anything that would cause Kent to make fun of them.

Tully ordered fried chicken for Donna Dee and himself. Latina could see the disdain in Kent's face as he ordered the seafood gala for the two of them. His silence as they ate bordered on sullenness that Latina wanted to shake out of him.

After eating, Kent took her to dance on the terrace overlooking the lake. A small stringed orchestra kept up a flow of romantic dance tunes. Taking her in his arms, he said, "Bruisers like Clouse are usually afraid of their own shadow. You know, the bigger they are, the harder they fall."

Oh Kent! She thought. Don't make matters worse. But she realized Kent was seeing Tully as she had that first week. How could he know Tully would brave a raging storm to rescue a silly rain-soaked stranger, or that he would give up his high school diploma for the sake of his little sister? "Sometimes that holds true; sometimes it doesn't."

"For Clouse, it's definitely the former."

Latina stepped back from his grasp. "It may interest you to know, Kent Starner, that I couldn't care less if Tully is afraid of his own shadow or not." Abruptly, she spun on her heel and strode to the railing at the edge of the dance floor.

Kent came briskly in pursuit. "Hey, Latina." His voice had softened. "Look, I'm sorry." He took hold of her arms and turned her around. "You can't blame a fellow for being a little jealous, can you? Here you are stuck out in the hills with a guy like that. He's not just your regular Joe, if you get my drift."

"I suppose I should be flattered," she told him. Truth was, she felt more threatened than flattered.

"So what's on the agenda for tomorrow, Sweetheart?" he asked, guiding her to a table there on the terrace.

Latina took a breath. "Let's fix a picnic and take it to the millpond."

"Somehow that doesn't sound too swinging. Tramping through mosquito-infested jungles just to see an old run-down mill. I'd sort of thought we could drive up to Springfield for the day."

Latina's heart plummeted. Her parents would never agree to her going that far alone with a boy—any boy. The dancers on the terrace swayed and glided to a melancholy tune that seeped into her consciousness and made her want to cry.

"We could shop in the afternoon and stay for a concert in the evening. Something's certain to be popping up there. What say?"

"It's out of the question, Kent. My parents would never let me go that far on a date." She dared not look at his face. Instead she stared out at the black velvety waters where lights from the shoreline glistened their reflections. Fingering one of the dangling earrings she wondered what he must think of her. A child? Immature?

"Our friends will think we've left them behind," she said, struggling to keep her voice steady.

"Not a bad idea," came his gruff reply.

Donna Dee brightened when she saw them returning. "Welcome back. We thought you'd jumped ship."

Latina prayed her cheeks were not as flushed as they felt, for Tully's searching eyes were looking clear through her.

"Guess we'll call it a night, gang," Kent announced making no move to reseat himself at the table. He picked up the check from beside his plate. "Separate checks? Where's the other one, Clouse? I'll catch it. This one's on me."

Tully patted his shirt pocket. "Appreciate the offer, but it's done."

Latina could barely think of him spending that precious money he'd worked so hard to earn. Jayleen and Althea needed so many things—he couldn't afford to spend it on senseless outings. This wild comedy of errors was making her more miserable by the minute.

"But Clouse," Kent was protesting. "I didn't want... I didn't think..." The more he struggled the more obvious it became that he assumed Tully had no money.

Tully's laughing eyes crinkled at the corners. He leaned close and whispered, "It's stash money what them revenooers ain't tuk from me yet. Don't you go squealing on me now, y'hear?"

Donna Dee's laughter rang out. "Oh Tully, you sound exactly like Grandpa Gar."

"The guy's a real scream," Kent muttered in Latina's ear as he pushed her firmly toward the cash register.

The drive back to Zell's Bush was relatively quiet, except for Tully and Donna Dee making soft conversation in the back seat. After letting them off at the sawmill, Latina and Kent were followed by Tully's noisy pickup as they drove over the inclines and around the bridges to the Nettleton farm, where Tully lumbered past them, giving a farewell *beep beep*.

Latina wondered if Kent would want to take a walk in the moonlight. It was such a beautiful evening. It would give her a chance to say something to ease the strain of the evening.

But without a word, he helped her from the car and led her up the front steps and in the door where her parents were waiting up, playing some sort of silly board game. If only they had gone to bed, then she could have talked to him immediately. Instead, he excused himself and retired to his room.

"Have a good time?" her mother wanted to know.

"Just great," she answered, and headed up the stairs to her room closing the door behind her.

Tomorrow she would ask them if she could go to Springfield. They might say yes. On the other hand, after resting and thinking about it, Kent might change his mind and want to go see the millpond after all. Once he saw the sun sparkling on the water and the rainbows dancing in the hanging mist, he'd love it as much as she did.

The next morning, she was awakened by Kent's muffled voice on the phone at the foot of the stairs. She dressed quickly and ran downstairs where she found Kent about to step out of his room. His luggage was sitting neatly by the door.

"Oh, Latina. There you are." His tone was distant. "I'm sorry. I was just calling my folks and guess what's happened?"

"I couldn't. Suppose you tell me."

"My dad wants me to get out to the coast right away. Something's come up and he needs me. I'll have to leave right after breakfast."

CHAPTER EIGHT

Kent's eyes averted hers as he loaded his luggage and climbed into the now-dusty rental car. She was glad he didn't say something dumb like, "It's been great seeing you," or "Hope we can do it again sometime," or even "I'll be seeing you." He simply said, "I'm sorry, Latina. Good-bye."

She watched the dust rise as the car made its way down the gravel drive before she returned to the house to strip the bed and throw out the wilted flowers. From now until September, it would be a matter of survival. The one dream she'd counted on to sustain her for the summer had gone up in smoke. She never expected to hear from Kent Starner again—ever.

Strangely enough, she sought refuge in the bosom of the hills. Almost daily, she packed a sandwich and a thermos, and carried her art paraphernalia to the solitude of the millpond. She couldn't bear to be around her family. They were probably thinking it was best that Kent left. After all, they hadn't liked him in the first place.

Over and over again, she rehearsed the two days of his stay, struggling to figure out what went wrong. If only she'd welcomed him with open arms the moment he appeared at the door. Then he might not have given Tully a second thought. But the damage was done. She'd never forgive herself for the mess she'd made.

Her painting no longer engaged her as it had before. Often, she simply sat on the rock overhang, staring and thinking. A noisy mockingbird had been a frequent visitor to her retreat, many times daring to come down on the lowest boughs of the willows. One afternoon as she was munching on her sandwich, he chanced to come down on the rock on which she was sitting. She tossed him bits of bread which he devoured. Before tossing more, she grabbed her sketchbook and quickly drew his charcoal-colored body, studying closely the vivid black trim on his wings and tail. The bird came to life through the pen in her hand.

He continued to share her lunches with her and was later joined by a squirrel who was also looking for a handout. Could they sense, as Althea had, that she was no threat? The animals trusted Tully; it seemed they trusted her as well.

Tully had received his first lessons back in the mail and was on his way to receiving his diploma. Latina, however, avoided talking to him, paying little attention to his comings and goings. Her mother had stepped into the role of personal teacher and chief support.

Donna Dee was Latina's only confidant. The two enjoyed long walks together, as well as more domestic activities, such as shelling peas, husking sweet corn, and breaking up "snap" beans—which Latina learned were just plain old green beans.

One evening they were sitting on the Garwood's front porch watching the sunset glowing through the trees. Latina had been talking of her painting when Donna Dee said, "I've told Daddy about your work and he says he'll pay you to do a picture of the sawmill and the house and all. What do you think?"

When Latina didn't answer for a moment, her friend added, "It may not look like much to some people." She made a sweeping wave with her arm. "But he's proud of every square inch."

Latina thought about it. Could she really paint something that would please Mr. Garwood? Finally, she answered, "Actually, I'm not that good. I'm just a novice. He needs a professional to do the job for him."

"How's about if you let Daddy judge? Do up some sketches for him, then he can say yes or no."

So it was by invitation that Latina found herself a few days later sitting on the hill opposite the sawmill rather than at her millpond. In the clearing where she sat, she had a bird's eye view of the valley. She surveyed the scene and wondered if it were possible to capture something for which she had little appreciation or interest.

Under the big sheds the saws screamed. The Garwood's small house sat rakishly on the hillside off to the side, connected only by the worn path that wound down the hill. On the far side of the house lay Etta Ann's garden, lush and green under the summer sun. Out near the sawdust piles stood a brick toolshed with its peaked roof. Everything was disjointed and scattered. No order to anything. A deep sigh escaped her lips. She just as well go down and tell Mr. Garwood right now that she could never pull this off.

A low rumble announced the arrival from out of the hills of a semitrailer loaded with logs. The mill sprang to life as Mr. Garwood shouted instructions to the men for unloading. The movements prompted her hands and mind as she sketched the activity around the truck. By noon, three false starts were lying in wadded clusters around her and the fourth attempt was beginning to come together.

At the sound of the noon whistle, the workers congregated under the shade trees near the sawdust piles to eat lunch. Latina rummaged in her bag for her own lunch. Presently, she saw Tully walking toward his pickup and getting his books and papers, evidently planning to study as he ate. He settled back against the trunk of a nearby tree.

"Just take a gander at old Clouse over there, fellas," she heard Collier say. The words were distinct in the warm summer air in spite of the distance from her spot on the hillside to the mill. "Thinks he's better than us just 'cause he reads some old words on paper. Ain't that the foolest notion you ever heard of?"

From what Latina could make out the other men were ignoring the outburst. But the dark-haired boy wasn't satisfied. Jumping to his feet, he stepped over to where Tully was sitting and grabbed papers from Tully's lap. "Let's just see what you got there, Professor Clouse. You been hanging with them city folk at Nettleton's so much y'all beginning to think like them."

Tully reached out to grab the papers, but not quickly enough. He said something that was inaudible to Latina.

Collier's high-pitched voice, however, was quite clear. "Now don't get yourself in an all-fired tizzy, cousin. I just want to check this stuff out, to see you're doing it proper like."

Latina's fists clenched as she watched the drama unfold. How she longed to see Tully flatten his cousin and shut him up once and for all.

"You can't read them papers, nohow, Hunsecker," one of the workers hooted.

"Could so," he countered sharply, "but who wants to? It's just a bunch of dumb trash!" Then like a vengeful child,

Collier ripped the pages in his hands and tossed them to the wind.

Silently, Tully rose, walked to the dusty blue pickup, got inside, and sat there reading a book.

"Don't worry, Clouse," Collier shouted after him. "It don't take no smarts to raise up a dim-witted sister."

Latina was incensed. How could Tully let Collier get away with such behavior? Had Kent been right about Tully being afraid of his own shadow? It seemed he couldn't even stand up to his cousin. Well, there was nothing much she could do about it. She gathered up her materials and started for home.

That evening, she bent over the sketches at her desk. She fleshed out the faint marks she'd made of the sawmill that afternoon. No breeze came in from the open window and her blouse clung to her back. She massaged her tired neck and shoulders with her fingertips. It was time for a break.

Slipping into the kitchen, she poured a glass of lemonade. From the porch, she could hear her mother talking to Tully, who was wresting one of the screens from its place. "Will you be ready to mail that composition by tomorrow, Tully?" she asked.

Tully's answer was slow in coming. "Looks like it'll be a few more days, ma'am."

"But I thought you were nearly finished."

"Something came up," Tully called back over his shoulder as he carried the screen out to the sawhorse. He and the professor were attaching new screen wire to each frame.

Something came up all right, Latina agreed silently. A loathsome cousin named Collier came up. Came right up and destroyed the composition in two seconds flat.

Latina's bare feet stepped quietly on the cool linoleum floor as she replaced the pitcher in the refrigerator.

She heard Tully laugh. "Now don't you be giving me no gosh-awful dunce cap, mizz schoolmarm."

It was the same act he'd pulled with Kent, only Kent hadn't thought it very funny.

From out in the yard she heard her father say, "Don't forget, Paulie, this boy has more to do than just study."

"Of course, you're right," came her mother's reply. "I guess I'm just getting too anxious. I won't pressure you, Tully. You're doing a great job."

As Latina turned to go back up to her room, Tully's voice sounded from behind her. "Say there, Latina."

She thought she couldn't be seen, but he must have caught movement as she passed by the door. They'd hardly spoken since the infamous day at the lake.

"Hello," she said. "Working hard?"

"Your daddy sees to that. He's a slave driver."

"You don't seem to be suffering much."

"The only suffering he's experiencing is acute thirst," Pauline said. "I'll get more lemonade."

As Pauline stepped into the kitchen, Tully thrust his torso through the window opening where the screen had been removed. "Althea and I want to know if you and Dirk are ready to go on that picnic with us."

"When?"

"How about this Saturday?"

"I don't think we had anything planned," she answered carefully. As if she had any plans at all, ever.

"Saturday it is then."

Latina prayed her brother would make no wisecracks about Kent in front of Tully. She had planned to warn him about it, but at the very moment she thought to mention it, the blue pickup rumbled up the drive and she changed her mind. It would be just like him to say something just to irritate her.

Tully jumped out to greet them with his customary "Howdy."

Dirk opted to ride in the bed of the pickup and Althea crawled into Latina's arms, her head bobbing and her eyes bright with excitement. Clasped into her baby-fine hair were Latina's two barrettes.

Tully parked just off the bridge where Latina first discovered the path down to the water's edge. Jayleen had packed lunch in an oversized wicker basket which Dirk offered to carry.

The four of them followed the stream's pebbled path until the water widened out and forced them into the underbrush. She and Tully traded off carrying Althea. As they walked, Tully pointed out to Dirk which of the trees were water tupelos and which were water birches. He pointed out the dogwood, the red oak, the willows, and then the delicate ferns along the bank.

Latina let Althea walk a ways through a clearing, holding tightly to her hand. Jayleen had told her that Althea knew her way through the woods like a lumberman, but Latina didn't want to take any chances.

"Fwy! Fwy!" she squealed.

"A butterfly. Yes, Althea. It's a pretty butterfly," Latina answered.

Her attention diverted, she missed seeing Tully lunge toward Dirk, but she heard Dirk's heavy "Oof!" as the two of them hit the ground.

"What on earth...? Dirk, are you all right?"

"I think so." Slowly he sat up. "And I think I see..." He pointed a few feet from where his next steps would have taken him. There lay a wicked, yawning steel trap.

Latina gasped. It was the first one she'd ever seen in all her comings and goings.

"Sorry fella." Tully ruffled Dirk's hair, then gave him a hand up. "I had to get you stopped."

Grabbing a thick stick, Tully triggered the mechanism. The resounding crack sent a shudder through Latina. She hugged Althea.

"Collier's work?" she asked, venturing nearer.

"Yep," Tully replied, his eyes meeting her.

"Who's Collier?" Dirk demanded. "Must not be too smart if he leaves things like this lying around." He dangled the trap at the end of its chain, making a harsh rattling sound.

"Collier Hunsecker is my cousin, Dirk."

"Oh, sorry."

"That's okay. You're right. This isn't the time or the place to set traps."

Tully lifted Althea to his shoulders, allowing her laughter to mask the tension. But in her mind, Latina still envisioned the wicked trap and the sharp teeth. Supposing it had been triggered by helpless little Althea?

"Wow, sis!" Dirk gave a low whistle as they stepped from the curtain of trees to the millpond. "This is neat!"

Although he was obviously itching to cross over and explore the mill, he offered to keep an eye on Althea as lunch was being spread out on the large flat rocks beneath the overhand. His newfound manners surprised Latina.

Jayleen's touch was evident in the lunch of fried chicken, deviled eggs, and fresh fruit pies covered in golden flaky crust. At the bottom of the basket lay a note. "Latina, I love you. Thanks. Jayleen."

Latina glanced to see if Tully noticed her reading it, but he was rolling a large log up onto the rocks. "For my backrest," he explained.

Lunch filled even the bottomless Dirk. Her friend the mockingbird came down for his share. Althea's face was decorated with blackberry filling from her pie, which she ate with great skill. Latina observed how Tully helped her, but never prevented her from helping herself.

Later, Dirk received permission to explore the mill, and Althea curled up against Tully's chest and fell asleep.

As Latina gathered the lunch scraps and repacked the basket, she remembered the note and handed it over for Tully to see. "She means that, Latina. Says she never saw Althea take to anyone like she has to you.

"I love Althea, and she knows it. But Tully, I really think we should think of her safety—that trap..."

"I was keeping close watch. I don't miss much."

"Sometimes people are coming through here when you aren't keeping watch," she retorted.

"I'm on Collier's heels most of the time. Releasing what he's set."

"Not that time," she said. "Tully, it's wrong. How can you let him get away with it?"

"Collier's got a hurting way down deep inside that makes him mean. Not much you can do about a thing like that."

"That hurting—did it make him tear up your composition?" She stepped to the edge of the rocks, pulled off her shoes and socks and dangled her feet in the cold water.

"You don't miss much either."

She looked around him and smiled. "I just happened to be on the hill across the road doing sketches for Mr.

Garwood. I saw the whole thing. If you let him get away with things like that, it'll make him worse. You can't tolerate wrong behavior and hope it'll go away." She paused a moment, then asked. "What makes him so hateful anyway?"

"His own daddy did it to him long time ago."

"Where's his father now?"

"Long gone. Ran out on him and his mama and brothers. Just ran out. But not before he did a heap of hurting to Collier."

"How?"

Althea awakened then and came over to Latina, winding her thin arms about Latina's neck and snuggling up close. Tully then moved to sit beside Latina. "Collier's daddy, Rendy Hunsecker, was sweet on his own wife's sister. He was a sorry husband and father."

"His wife's sister?"

"My mama. Jayleen."

"Did she love him?"

Tully shook his head. "Nope. She had eyes only for Aaron Clouse." His voice went soft. "The world's greatest."

After a moment, he continued. "Collier's daddy always put me up to Collier without mercy. Always telling Collier he didn't do things as good as I did; asking him why he couldn't be more like me. My daddy told him it was wrong, but Uncle Rendy wouldn't listen. Loved Mama so much he was blind—and deaf to hearing truth.

"When my daddy passed on, Uncle Rendy showed up at our front door the day after the funeral telling us he was going to get a divorce and marry Mama right away." Tully gave a little snort. "When Mama pointed him to the road and told him never to come back, he went sort of crazy. Beat Collier up pretty bad, then disappeared. He's never been back."

Tully paused and reached over to stroke Althea's hair. "So you see, Collier can't look at me in a right light. He never will be able to because of his daddy making me his enemy all those years."

"Still, it's not fair," Latina said hotly. "Collier needs to be turned in and prosecuted for breaking the law."

"Could be. But I figure if you give a man enough rope he'll hang himself. Collier's trapping brings him money of his own. He feels it's his right since he's had such a rough time of things. I don't bother him much. Just take wounded animals that aren't dead and release traps that are near pathways.

Excited calls from Dirk interrupted their conversation. It was coming from behind them. "Tully! Latina! Hurry, come and look!"

Tully swept Althea up in his arms and Latina followed. Dirk was kneeling over a young raccoon whose leg was caught in the teeth of a steel trap. It appeared the poor creature had given up on struggling.

"Can you get him out, Tully?" Dirk asked with pleading eyes.

"Sure can. Move back a bit. Latina, take Althea."

It took several tries before Tully pressed open the trap. Within moments, the furry creature was safe in Dirk's arms. Before Latina could protest, Tully was ripping at his shirttail to create a bandage for the injured leg.

"Can I keep him?" Dirk asked.

"I don't see why not. You found him. I'll give you one of my cages. When his leg heals, you'll have a sweet little pet. He's still young enough you can tame him." Tully rubbed the raccoon's furry ear.

"Neat! Thanks, Tully."

Latina moved closer so she and Althea could touch the animal. She could feel the trembling of his little body. How cruel to harm such a helpless little creature.

Later in the afternoon, when the four of them emerged from the cool of the woods to the dusty road, a rusted out pickup came rumbling around the curve, rolling up a cloud of dust behind it. When the driver spied the small party beside the road, the vehicle came to a stop and Collier jumped out onto the bridge.

"Howdy, Tully," he said. "Where you been?" He spoke to Tully but his eyes were on Dirk and the furry bundle in his arms.

"We took Althea on a picnic," Tully answered, his voice even.

"Well, now. Looks like you been messing with my traps again. You ought not done that. You're gonna get yourself in a whole lot of trouble." Standing before Dirk, he glared at him. "Hand over my coon!"

Dirk stepped back. "He's mine. I found him."

"Any traps in that valley are mine. You got no call to be messing with my traps, kid. Now give him over."

With an easy grace, Tully stepped between the two of them. "Leave him alone, Collier. If it's coons you're wanting you know I got a whole barn full of them."

"Aw you're so uppity, Tully Clouse. Act like you're something special just 'cause you can read and study some. I'll get you for this, just you wait and see."

The tires of his truck spun in the gravel as he gunned the motor and barreled over the rattling bridge.

CHAPTER NINE

Latina stood at her bedroom window watching her father lay the wood for their Fourth of July backyard cookout. Her family had been pleased with her suggestion to invite the Garwoods, the Clouses, and the Boles over for the evening.

No doubt her parents would have just planned another fishing trip. How unimaginative. She felt a bit smug as she observed the preparations in progress. Tables had been constructed out of planks resting across sawhorses, and Etta Ann had provided brightly patterned tablecloths to cover them.

Perhaps this would be the night that Tully would really notice her, she thought as she brushed her hair until it fell softly around her shoulders. She wished they could begin again in their relationship and put the awful weekend with Kent behind them. After adding a touch of lipstick, and slipping her feet into her white sandals, she hurried downstairs.

The Garwoods had arrived first. She could hear the friendly conversation in the backyard as she stood at the sink cutting carrot sticks. Donna Dee was helping place food out on the table.

"Howdy, Latina," Tully said walking into the kitchen carrying the wicker picnic basket. "You sure look nice."

"Thank you, Tully." She felt her face grow warm. "All the food goes out back." She motioned toward the back door with a dripping hand, trying to think of something to say to keep him talking to her, but her mind went blank.

He moved on through to the back door, snitching a carrot stick on the way and giving her a smile. When she carried out the relish platter later, Tully was checking on the pet coon while Mr. Garwood looked on.

Once everyone arrived, the feasting began. Southern fried chicken, fried okra, creamed peas and new potatoes, roasting ears, homemade yeast rolls, and pies and cakes galore. Dirk opted to roast hot dogs over the fire. Latina had never seen so much food in one place.

After she helped with the serving, Latina took Althea to a lawn chair and helped her eat. As she wiped the girl's sticky fingers and smeared face, she wondered what would become of Jayleen and Althea after Tully left for college. Already, her mother had mentioned that he could apply for scholarships at Eagleton College. Perhaps it had been a mistake for her parents to interfere in this way. Her father had said that if Tully were able to find a job in Eagleton and had scholarship money, he could perhaps send money home to help Jayleen. But Latina wasn't sure that would be enough. Tully did the bulk of the shopping for the family, plus all the outdoor chores around the place.

Later the fire had burned down to a reddish-blue heap—perfect for roasting marshmallows. Dirk had a bulging pocket of firecrackers, but when asked about them, he explained he'd decided to wait until tomorrow to shoot them in case they might "disturb Althea."

Latina studied her long-legged brother, who must have grown at least two inches just since their arrival. She wondered if this could be the same boy who used to always insist on having his own way. Her entire family was changing, she thought as she saw her father move his chair closer to his wife and put his arm around her shoulder.

Was it the effect of the quiet beauty of the hills? Or the selfless fortitude of the people they had come to know? Perhaps both. She looked at Tully's strong face reflected in the glow of the fire.

He must have felt her gaze because he looked back and smiled. She wanted so much to know what he thought of her, yet she was afraid to ask.

After dark, Tully helped her father and Mr. Garwood with a small fireworks display in the front driveway. Shortly after the spectacle was over and they had returned to the backyard, Latina saw Tully walking with Donna Dee down the long driveway, their outlines barely visible in the moonlight. She suppressed the rising feelings of jealousy—just because she loved Donna Dee so much.

Althea was asleep in Jayleen's arms when the party began to break up. Latina helped carry the picnic basket to the pickup for her. Repeatedly, Jayleen thanked Latina for the evening. "I can't remember when I've had such a nice time. Before we lost Aaron, I suppose. You've been such a blessing, Latina."

"I'm glad you enjoyed yourself. It was fun having you," Latina told her, embarrassed by the praise.

"I wouldn't have missed it for all the world," she said as she settled herself and the sleeping Althea into the pickup.

"Me neither." Tully had come up behind them and overheard.

As he hopped in beside his mother, Jayleen said, "Oh, Latina. I just remembered something. Miss Wilkes, Althea's teacher, wants to meet you. I told her about how you made up to Althea so quick and she said she wanted to get to know you."

"Fine. Anytime. I'll be here." She was hoping Tully would say something about another picnic, but instead he was saying they better get on home because Althea was "plumb tuckered out."

For a time after the guests had left, Latina sat alone in the yard poking at the last of the glowing embers with one of the wiener-roasting sticks and staring at the fountain of sparks she created. Now that the evening had come and gone, it seemed almost anticlimactic. The entire thing had been her idea, and she knew everyone had a good time, but it had disturbed her to see Tully and Donna Dee together. If they were serious about one another, was Donna Dee planning to wait for Tully until he finished college?

She thought again about Kent. Now he seemed more a memory than a real person. She realized she'd never truly known him at all. They had never talked of things that mattered, but always chatted about surface things of no consequence.

But Tully... At what precise moment had her feelings about him changed? Was it when she saw his room filled with books and woodcarvings? Or the moment he saved Dirk from the trap? Perhaps it had been...

Just then, a sharp snap in the dense darkness ahead of her, past the glowing fire, gave her a start. Dropping the stick into the fire, she ran into the house and up to her room. Would she ever feel completely safe in the swallowing-up hills?

The next morning she awakened to her brother's anguished cries. Jumping out of bed, she grabbed her robe and slippers, ran down the stairs, out the back door onto the wet grass. She pushed past her parents to see Dirk's precious Coony lying on the grass. She turned away as soon as she saw the bloodied fur.

Her father took a closer look. "Someone pried open the clasp and stabbed the little thing."

Pauline had her arms around her son in an attempt to console him. "Who would do such a terrible thing?" she demanded.

"His name is Collier Hunsecker," Latina supplied the answer. "He's Tully's cousin. The same guy who set the trap that caught Coony in the first place." Then she remembered the noise that had startled her the night before and shivered. Had Collier been lurking there in the woods watching her?

Fighting not to cry, Dirk told how Collier had demanded the raccoon be given back to him. "I should have kept Coony on the back porch during the night," he said in a tight little-boy voice. "Then he would have been safe."

"Even if you had," Latina put in, "he would have found another way to get even. Collier's got a mad on all the time," she said, using Donna Dee's phrasing.

"Let's hope he's had his revenge now and leaves us alone," Pauline said.

"I know one thing for sure. I'm going to help Tully release every trap that Collier ever sets," Dirk threatened through clenched teeth. "That guy needs to be stopped."

When Tully learned of the incident a few days later, he apologized for Collier. "Don't hold him responsible," he told the Harmens. "He's bitter because he didn't get his own way. If you're willing to let Dirk have another pet, he can have the pick of what I have up at the barn. Collier never touches the ones I have. He knows better."

Although Tully's offer appeased Dirk and her parents, Latina couldn't forget Collier's act of cruelty. She thought of calling the local wildlife officials and turning him in. But if he found out who had made the call, what other dreadful thing would he do?

Shortly after the Fourth of July picnic on a Saturday morning, Latina was in the Garwood's living room with the initial sketches spread out on the large oval dining room table.

Etta Ann flitted about, getting glasses of cold cider and peering over her husband's shoulder at the sketches and muttering, "My my, would you look at that."

Latina had hoped Donna Dee would be there to act as a liaison, but Etta Ann explained that she'd gone to the Clouse's for a visit.

When the decision was made on which pictures she should pursue, Latina left quickly—glad to get out from under the pressure. She'd never had to show her work to anyone before—other than family, that is.

As she was getting in the car, Donna Dee drove up. "Latina," she called out, "did he like them?"

"Sort of, I guess. At least he wants me to go ahead on a couple"

Her friend was by her side now taking the sketches from her hand. "Let's see." She looked from one to the next. "These are good, Latina. If you only knew how hard it is to please Daddy with things like this, you'd know it's more than 'sort of' with him."

"You really think so?"

"I know so. And you're such a hit with Althea, too. All she can talk about is 'Ah-teen-a.'"

Latina smiled. "The feeling's mutual."

"It's great for Jayleen, too. Not many people around here accept Althea like you have. It's not their fault, of course. They have old-fashioned ideas that if someone has a child who doesn't act right, they ought to hide them away."

"That's hard on Jayleen, isn't it?"

Donna Dee nodded. "Very hard."

"I've thought about helping," Latina confided, "but I don't want to barge in."

"She's up there alone with Althea every day. You can be sure you'd be welcome anytime you went to visit. I used to go up more often before I started working." After a moment, she added, "Have you heard that Miss Wilkes wants to meet you?"

"Jayleen told me the other evening. At first, I was doubtful, but now I'm anxious to meet her as well. I've wondered what type of person travels into the hills to help a handicapped child."

"You'll like her. She's a sweet person, just like you."

Before leaving, Latina gave her friend an affectionate hug. As she drove home she once again thought of how her friendship with this backwoods girl had literally saved her summer.

Later that afternoon, she was sitting out in the front yard in the shade of the oaks, preparing to sketch the old farmhouse. She flipped though her sketchbook and realized that her style was improving, but she still needed guidance and instruction. It had never occurred to her to study art, but now it didn't seem like such a bad idea. Possibly she could fit it into her fall schedule. She'd talk to her mother about it.

One picture in her book was of Tully and Dirk preparing the cage for Coony. She'd been out in the yard in one of the metal lawn chairs watching them work. At first, she attempted to draw the raccoon's masked face, which she did fairly successfully. But then she found herself sketching out Tully's square jaw and his thick sandy hair. The mouth wasn't too great a challenge, nor was his straight nose, but his eyes—what pencil or brush could ever capture the caring and the understanding in those clear, blue eyes?

She was busily sketching the outline of the house when a strange car pulled in. The light film of dust proclaimed that it wasn't a local. The driver, a young lady, waved at her. As Latina left her place on the spread-out blanket and walked to the car, the lady called out through the open window, "Are you Latina Harmen?"

"That's me."

"I'm Beverly Wilkes, Althea's tutor."

She much younger than Latina had imagined. They shook hands through the car window. "I'd like to talk to you if you have a minute."

"I have all the time in the world. Let me grab my stuff."

After putting the blanket and her sketch books in the back seat and getting in the car, Latina surveyed the stranger with interest. Her light-brunette hair was brushed back from her face in a casual style, and she was dressed in lightweight slacks and sleeveless blouse. The Keds on her feet made her look like a college student. She immediately won Latina's approval.

After introductions were made with her parents, her father returned to his study, and Miss Wilkes sat in the front room with Latina and Pauline.

Miss Wilkes came right to the point. "From what Jayleen tells me, you have an affinity with Althea, Latina. It would seem you have an almost natural talent for working with such children."

"I've not been around them that much. All I know is that Althea is easy to love, and that the Clouses do a great job of teaching her."

"You're very perceptive, Latina. However, even with the insight they possess, they're still isolated with the child. Most of the townspeople aren't supportive or sympathetic toward them and Jayleen gets lonely."

Her comments only confirmed what Donna Dee had said earlier. Miss Wilkes continued. "It occurred to me that Jayleen might attempt to take Althea on a shopping trip if you were there to help. Or perhaps even out to lunch in Palatka."

Latina's eyes caught her mother's. Pauline was beaming.

"I've wanted to help them, Miss Wilkes." Latina turned her attention back to their guest, "but I didn't know how."

"Please, call me Beverly. I was fairly certain you'd agree." The joy in Beverly's face indicated more than a casual interest in this student. "You're an unselfish girl, Latina, and I know you'll be enriched for having helped them. But I'm sure you already know that."

Jayleen was shaking her head. "I'm just not sure, Latina. Being with Althea here at home or out in the woods is different than taking her into a crowd. People stare. They whisper. It's hard."

"But I'll be there to help you. You can shop and I'll stay with her in the car. Then we can meet Donna Dee for lunch. We'd only spend a few hours. It could be a small start for you."

Latina looked over where Althea was in the corner playing with her favorite doll. "Someday she'll be out in the world more than ever. Wouldn't this be the best time to prepare her?" Latina asked.

"You're right, of course. I'm grateful for your offer. I guess I just an old fraidy-cat. Give me a minute to get myself ready."

Within the hour the three set off. Latina was thankful their car had air conditioning because the day was hot, still, and muggy. Althea's balance was such that Jayleen had to carry her on her lap the entire way. Latina knew that task in itself was enough to tire out anyone. Althea bounced and wiggled and jabbered, seeming to sense that something special was in store.

Jayleen made several purchases at several different stores. At first, Latina stayed in the car with Althea, but later with Jayleen's permission, she took her into the grocery store. Latina marveled at her alertness and eagerness to learn. Although her speech was badly slurred, Latina was learning to interpret.

The last stop before they meet Donna Dee for lunch was the hardware store. As Latina waited with Althea in the car, Althea accidently bumped the car's horn. Latina chuckled at the surprise that registered on the little girl's face. She studied the steering wheel intently as though searching where the sound came from. Her clumsy hands explored the steering wheel.

Carefully, Latina took hold of the small hand and guided it to press on the horn. At the sound, Althea's face lit up with excitement. She knew she'd done it. She had made the noise work. Suddenly, it became a game that Latina wasn't sure she could stop.

Presently, Jayleen came out to the car and took Althea onto her lap. "Getting impatient?" she asked.

"Would you believe it? That was your daughter!" Latina explained how easily Althea followed her instructions. They were still laughing over the incident when they entered the cool recesses of the restaurant.

Donna Dee was holding a table for them, and after ordering sandwiches and salads, they enjoyed some girl talk. Althea sat in a toddler's seat with her thin legs hanging past the footrest. She smiled and babbled happily, relishing every bite of her lunch.

Later, Donna Dee rushed back to her office and Latina and Jayleen loaded Althea into the car to return to the hills. It had been a good day and a landmark for Jayleen.

"I would never in a million years have mustered up the courage to go without your help," she told Latina as together they carried Jayleen's purchases into the house. "I don't know how I could ever thank you. You came into our lives at just the right time. To think we have Miss Wilkes helping us, and now you. I keep pinching myself to see if I'm dreaming."

When she arrived home, Latina found her father in the front room with a lap full of file folders. "Hi, Latina. How was your day in the big city?"

"We had a great day—that is, if you were referring to Palatka as the *big city.*" Flopping into a nearby chair she described their day.

Her father leaned back listening intently. "Latina, I have to say, I'm quite impressed by what you're doing for the Clouses."

"Thanks, Dad. It's just that it doesn't seem like anything special." She stood to her feet. "Now I'm going upstairs to change into a pair of cool shorts before I melt."

"By the way," her father said, going back to the folders in his lap. "I've been smelling paint fumes coming from the room next to mine. I do believe Parke Garwood has seen more of your work than I have. Being secretive, are we?"

"You've been a little secretive, too," she retorted waving at the stacks of files and papers strewn about.

He lifted a bulging file from his lap. "There are some fascinating things in here. Would it interest you to know that it was Tully's great-grandfather who built the old mill with its elegant waterwheel?"

Latina slowly lowered herself back into her chair. "I'd be *very* interested," she replied. "And what about the Nettletons? Have you dug up anything about them?"

"As a matter of fact, I have. But I asked first." He stood and reached for her hand. "Let's go see your paintings."

Having the professor review her work was more unsettling than presenting them to Mr. Garwood. After all, Mr. Garwood simply wanted to see his sawmill on canvas.

"Mm," her father mumbled around his pipe stem. "Mm. Hm." He lingered over the sketches and paintings. There were several of the millpond, two of the sawmill and various ones of the house and other scenes that had caught her eye. The one of Tully was purposely hidden under her bed. That was hers alone.

"Latina, these are good."

She let her breath out slowly.

"In fact, they're very good." He held his pipe and looked at her. "So good that I'd like to ask your permission to submit a few of them along with my manuscript to use as possible illustrations for the book."

Latina could hardly believe what she was hearing. After she realized he wasn't kidding, she said, "I'd be honored to be associated with such a fine historian, Professor Harmen." She threw her arms around his neck.

"Now then," he said, clearing his throat, "come and see what I've uncovered. Some of these things will astound you."

That evening, Latina browsed through file after file of notes her father had collected about Zell's Bush and its people. As she read, she marveled at the courage and the stamina of the ones who'd settled in this rugged land. Knowing some of their descendants personally, she could see how the courage still flowed in their veins.

She had come to a new appreciation of her father's work—and now she had an opportunity to have a small part in it.

CHAPTER TEN

The cool of the millpond was delightfully refreshing. The intense July heat had not even penetrated the protective veil of trees. Latina could hear shouts of laughter coming from down by the falls where Dirk had taken Althea to wade in the shallow water.

Turning from her easel, she looked at Tully stretched out in the sun, napping on the smooth rocks. She thought of how Dirk had been influenced by Tully: now he too had become sensitive to Althea's needs and demands.

Latina's imagination had been working overtime for the past week, dreaming of how she might respond if Tully invited her for another picnic. However, it was Jayleen who suggested it.

"The little one's been raring to go on another picnic, Latina," Jayleen said a few days earlier. "Could you and Dirk go this Saturday? I know it'd be fine with Tully."

When Tully had arrived to pick them up, she was still wrestling with questions of where his feelings for her actually stood. Now whenever he smiled at her, her heart did crazy, wild things, and her mouth went cottony dry. He had never once given any indication of affection toward her other than appreciation for her help with Althea. Why then the unexplainable ache within her? The intense longing to see him and hear his soft voice speak her name? It was all so crazy.

She squinted against the sunlight filtering through the dense trees, which had transformed the water to a rare shade of emerald. Swirling her brush in the greens of her palette, she struggled to duplicate the scene on canvas.

Presently, Tully roused himself and grinned sheepishly as though embarrassed at having fallen asleep.

"Welcome back," she said.

"Too much good food and warm sun. An icy dip will fix that." He retreated behind the boulders to strip to his swim trunks before mounting the higher rocks and diving into the water. Surfacing, he called for her to join him.

"Just a sec," she replied, wanting to finish a bit more before stopping.

When it came her turn a few minutes later, her dive into the frigid spring water lacked the gracefulness of his, and she was gasping from cold as her head bobbed up. "Feels like the North Sea!" she said between clenched teeth.

"You'll get used to it."

"Your dive was flawless," she told him.

"Dad taught me. We used to spend hours here together."

"He must have been a great swimmer."

"The best."

"Will you show me what I'm doing wrong?"

"I'd be obliged."

Together they climbed back up on the rocks and he pointed out the weaknesses in her form and push-off. Later, they swam closer to the mill where she could see the huge waterwheel and how it had been constructed. As she gazed upward, suddenly, without warning, she felt herself being dragged under water without a split second to swallow a precious gulp of air. Sucked down, down, down. Stabbing pains jabbed into her chest. An eternity of spinning, and sinking, and blackness and pain and fear. Surely her lungs were going to burst.

A strong arm wound tightly around her neck, squeezing and jerking and pulling upward. In an explosion of air, she burst to the surface gasping to breathe. Coughing and sputtering, she clung to Tully as he lifted her up to the bank. Placing her carefully on a sun-baked rock he kneeled beside her.

"Whirlpool," he said. "It happened too fast to warn you. Sorry."

Gradually, she began to breathe more evenly. He placed his hands over hers. "I almost..." his voice caught. "I almost lost you."

Through half-closed eyes she saw his face come close to hers. She felt his lips gently brush her forehead. "Latina-Flower, you gave me a terrible fright."

"That makes twice you've had to rescue me," she barely had time to whisper before Dirk exploded on the scene.

"Hey, you guys. What happened?"

⁂

"Let's go out to the garden and pick your mama a mess of tomatoes," Donna Dee said to Latina one evening after she had arrived at the Garwood home. Then in a low whisper, she said, "I need to talk to you private-like. Alone! Now!"

"Oh sure," Latina agreed glancing over toward the kitchen where Etta Ann was busy at the stove. "Mom would love some more tomatoes."

When they reached the garden, Latina saw that Donna Dee had no sack for the tomatoes. "What's ailin' you, child?" she said in a friendly imitation of Etta Ann's voice. "You're actin' all addle pated."

Donna Dee laughed a little and took a deep breath. "Latina, do you believe in love at first sight?"

"At first sight?" Latina paused, remembering how she had despised Tully when she first looked on his laughing eyes that day in Boles' Grocery. "I don't know. I suppose it *could* happen."

"It has, Latina! It has—to me!"

"*You?*"

"Yes, me. Of all people." She took a little whirl down the row of tall trellised tomatoes. "Brad Jenner and I are in love. On Latina, he's so wonderful. So wonderful." She came dancing back to Latina's side. "I know he's the right one for me. And look." From her jeans pocket she drew out the most delicate diamond ring Latina had ever seen. She slipped it on her ring finger and held it up to admire how it sparkled in the last rays of sunlight.

"You and Brad? But what about you and Tully?" The cry of her heart tumbled out of her mouth before she could stop it.

"Tully? You thought I was sweet on Tully? Honey, I'm a full two years older than that boy. He's like my younger brother. Why, I've known him all my life."

She placed her hand gently on Latina's arm. "I've noticed the way you look at him lately, though. I guess this really *is* good news, isn't it."

Latina blushed. "Hey we're getting off the subject. You're the one all giddy and cow-eyed."

Latina thought back to the night of the Fourth when she saw the two of them walking together. Donna Dee was probably telling him all about Brad Jenner.

"Listen, Latina," Donna Dee was saying, "I'm going to need your support. The law firm has decided to move Brad and his cousin upstate to open another office and Brad will be leaving." She stopped and smiled. "He's asked me to marry him before he leaves. I don't know what Mama and Daddy will say. They might think I can't be sure in such a short time."

Latina started to object, unsure how she could ever help, but Donna Dee kept talking.

"But I'm sure of this decision. More sure than I've ever been in my life. All I'm asking is for you to stay with me till I tell them. Would you do that for me? You've been such a dear to me this summer. I've never had a friend so close. Not even all through high school."

Latina gave her friend a hug. "You're the greatest, Donna Dee. It's no wonder that young lawyer lost his heart over you. I bet he still doesn't know what hit him."

It was Donna Dee's turn to blush. "Well, are you with me or not?"

"Through thick and thin." Hooking her arm through Donna Dee's, they walked back to the house.

❧◉❧

"Mother, you'll never guess what," Latina said, pulling up a chair beside her mother and collapsing into it. "Donna Dee's gone and fallen in love with the young lawyer in her office, and she's getting married right away. We're all invited to the wedding. It's to be a small ceremony at the Zell's Bush Community Church.

"Whoa. Wait a minute," her mother protested, placing the afghan that she was crocheting into the large tapestry bag at her feet. "Slow down and begin at the beginning. You're going too fast."

To begin at the beginning, Latina thought, would mean telling how she had thought that Donna Dee and Tully were more than just friends, and how excited she was to learn that wasn't true at all. But this wasn't the right time to tell it. As briefly as possible, she told Donna Dee's news.

She worried about what her mother would think of such a short courtship, but was relieved to hear her say, "Why, that's wonderful news! I'm pleased the girl is marrying someone who can support her. So many of the young people in this area seem to be trapped here. But I could tell Donna Dee was different."

"Like Tully?"

"Like Tully." Her mother gazed for a moment out past the backyard into the trees behind the Nettleton house. "That Tully's a whiz. He's covering material quickly. He'll be ready for college by the second semester at least."

"Mom, why haven't you and Dad encouraged Tully to attend a college nearer home?"

Pauline thought for a moment. "Well, it's because we felt since we would both be there at Eagleton, we could give him more assistance than if he were among strangers. In the end, the decision is his to make. He's looked at the brochures and catalogs we've shown him and seems to love the idea."

But what would college do to his personality? Latina wondered. How would he endure dorm life after roaming the untamed hills, nursing wild animals, and diving from the rocks at the millpond? And who would save the animals from the clutches of the steel traps?

"You're not too sure about all this are you, dear?"

"It's Jayleen," she replied. That was partly true. Pausing for a moment, she added, "Mom, could we buy them a gift to help out?"

"Gift? What kind of gift?"

"I've been thinking about how difficult it is for them to travel with Althea and I thought a car booster seat might help."

Pauline smiled. "That's a great idea, Latina. She's bigger than a toddler though. We'd have to get a sturdy one."

"Would it be expensive?" Latina knew their finances had been tight that summer.

"It would, but I think your father would feel it's worth it. And I agree wholeheartedly."

"Can we shop for it tomorrow? I'd like you to help me pick it out."

"It's a date!"

⚜

On the way to Palatka the next day, Latina found herself opening up and sharing more with her mother than she had for a long time. Especially when the subject turned to her painting.

"There's still so much I don't know." Latina had kicked off her sandals and sat curled up in the rider's side. It felt good to have her mother negotiating the hills for a change. She'd never gotten used to the hairpin curves. "I was wondering if I could fit an art class into my fall schedule."

"That's a great idea. We can call the school and see what's available."

Latina stared at the trees whipping past. "I'm going to miss everyone a lot," she admitted.

"We all are." Pauline turned a tight curve while meeting a logging truck grinding its gears. Then she added, "The summer turned out better than you'd first thought, right?"

Latina nodded. "I've learned so much about so many things. Just meeting Althea has been an experience in itself."

"You're quite taken with her, aren't you."

"She's so easy to love. I keep thinking there must be scores of children like her everywhere who need someone to understand them."

Without planning to, she spoke the thought that had been growing in her mind. "Mom, I'd like to be like Beverly Wilkes—someone who's there to help and to understand. I want to learn how to teach children like Althea. I like how Beverly not only teaches Althea, but helps Jayleen as well."

For the first time in her life Latina felt a sense of purpose. It was an exhilarating discovery.

Rosie, the coon hound, silently padded up to Latina and licked her hand as she stepped up to the Clouse's front door. Tully answered her knock. "Latina-Flower. Come on in here. Althea's napping, but I can wake her. It's about time anyway."

"No," she told him. "Not yet."

"Come on in," Jayleen called to her from the far side of the kitchen. "So pleased to see you again."

"I, uh, I've brought a little something for you. It's in the car." Suddenly she wondered if she'd assumed too much. The Clouses were a proud family, not given to receiving charity. Would they think she felt sorry for them? Perhaps she should have asked first. Tully might even think she'd bought a gift just to impress him.

"You have something for us, you say?" Jayleen was at the door now, wiping her hands on a faded dish towel. "Wherever could it be?"

"You'll see." Looking up at Tully, she said. "It's in the trunk. I'll need your help."

"I'm with you." He followed her out into the warm evening.

She hoped he didn't detect the trembling in her fingers as she turned the key in the trunk lock. As the dim light of the trunk illuminated the large box, decorated with the obvious pictures of the contents, Tully was suddenly silent.

"It's for Althea." Her words were barely above a whisper. "From our family to yours. So Jayleen can take her places by herself."

She forced herself to turn now and look up at him. "Um, you'll have to carry it. It's pretty awkward." It was then she saw the tears glistening in his eyes.

"Latina-Flower, you tell your fine family that we're mighty grateful. Mighty grateful."

He still stood there for another long moment staring at the box. She was amazed at his unashamedness at free-flowing tears. Unbidden her hand reached up to bush away a tear. The ached within her to touch him was overwhelming.

He reached out and took her hand and pressed it again his face. "Let's go show Mama!" he said suddenly, lifting up the box and closing the trunk with a slam.

Jayleen too shed tears of joy as she opened the box. "Latina, we're so grateful. Whoo, it's a pretty one, isn't it?" Tully gave her a hand pulling it out of the box. "There's no way we could ever say thanks good enough for all this."

"You already have, Jayleen. By just being yourselves. I've learned so much from having known you."

"Oh pawsh. We're just common folk. But this—this is so grand." She ran her fingers over the padded seat. "Won't it be grand to have Althea ride in this, Tully? Why we could even set her in it here in the house. Won't she be as fine as any little girl sitting in this?" With that, she set it up on the couch.

"It's perfect, Mama," Tully agreed. "Perfect."

As his mother busied herself with the car seat, Tully turned to Latina. "I've got to drive up to Campton Corners this evening to get some parts for Garwood's saw from another mill. In fact, I should have left before now. What to ride along?"

"Why, I'd love to," she managed to say above the beating in her heart.

Their conversation along the way was easy and light. Tully asked several questions about Eagleton College that she was unable to answer, even though she'd lived near the campus all her life. It struck her how she'd taken for granted that college would be her destination. For Tully, it was still an intangible dream.

"How will Jayleen manage once you're gone?" She finally mustered up the courage to ask the question she'd wrestled with for weeks.

"We've talked about it a lot. I guess leaving her alone with Althea will be about the hardest thing I've ever done. But your parents are opening a door for me that I thought was closed forever. If I don't go through it now, I may miss the chance completely." He glanced over at her. "To my way of thinking, a college education will better equipment to help them even more on down the road."

Of course that made so much sense; sacrifice now to gain the benefits later. Tully's good sense at work.

"You'll still be here in the summer?"

"I think so. But winters are hardest. Keeping the wood cut and all."

"Can't some of the neighbors help?"

"Some will, but that's not enough. I'll have to see to it that the supply is in before I leave. A full winter's supply."

"What does Jayleen say about your leaving?"

"She's tickled pink. She's been pushing me to go from the first moment I mentioned it. 'We'll get along,' she says. 'The Lord'll watch over us every day. You wait and see.'"

Latina could just hear her saying it. "She's little but mighty, isn't she?"

He thought about that for a moment. "I reckon she is, Latina. I reckon she is."

Campton Corners was a town much like Zell's Bush. Parke Garwood had called ahead with the request. It took only a few minutes to talk to the mill owner and get the needed part.

On the way home, Tully pulled up to a gas station where the lights out front wore hazy yellow halos. Through the dust-dimmed window, Latina saw him feeding coins into a decrepit pop machine. As she lay her head back on the pickup seat, she thought that even in the smartest places that Periwinkle Cove had to offer, she'd never been this happy.

He opened the creaking pickup door and handed her a chilled can of soda and slid behind the wheel. Once out on the road, he surprised her by asking. "So what do you hear from that guy back East? Old what's-his-name."

She hadn't thought of Kent for weeks. "You mean Kent."

"Oh yeah. Kent it was. You hear from him?"

"Um…" She took a sip of cold soda and felt it sting up to her nose.

"Well?"

"Well what?"

"About hearing from that Kent fellow."

"I haven't heard," she admitted.

"Not at all?"

"Not at all."

"Not even a little note? Or a card? Or a phone call?"

"Not a line. Not a word."

Tully maneuvered the hills deftly while nursing his soda. Then he said, "You think I upset him?"

Boy did you, she wanted to say. And so did I. She waited a minute before answering. Awkwardly, she caught the door handle so she wouldn't slide across the seat as he took a sharp hairpin curve a little too fast.

"Something must have upset him," she offered.

"He upset easily?"

"I hadn't thought so—until he came to Zell's Bush."

"Zell's Bush has a refining fire you go through. Tests the mettle to see what you're made of. Some just can't handle it." His eyes were laughing now. She could see them by the reflection of the dash lights.

"Are you the refining fire?"

"Me? Heavens no! It's the hills."

"The hills, huh?"

"They make you or break you."

Don't they though? She thought back to how ominous and threatening they had been to her at the beginning. "And what about me?" she wanted to know. "Has my mettle been refined in the fire?"

"Latina." His voice was soft again. "You've passed with flying colors."

At that moment, another corner caught her unawares, causing her to slide and fall over against him. Tossing his empty pop can to the floor, he freed his hand to place an arm around her and pull her closer.

"Are we gonna have to get you a car seat like Althea's to hold you in?" he asked. "Or do you mind if I do the job?"

She could only smile and snuggle closer.

CHAPTER ELEVEN

Latina attempted to read Parke Garwood's reactions to her paintings by watching his eyes. They were sitting in the Garwood's living room and the canvases, now mounted in oak frames, were propped up on the coffee table. That is Etta Ann and Latina were sitting; Mr. Garwood was pacing.

Presently, he stopped and looked at the paintings once again, then spoke. "We're obliged to you, Latina. When I look at the mill in a picture like this, it sorta gives me a broader outlook on things. Like getting outta my skin and looking at myself to get things figured out in my head. Know what I mean?"

Latina knew exactly what he meant. She'd been going a great deal of soul searching herself the past few weeks. But she only nodded.

"These are fine paintings. Our family will put a lot of store by these for many years to come. Don't know how to tell you how much it means to us."

Latina could think of nothing to say in reply, but Mr. Garwood wasn't done.

"And more that all that, I'm mighty proud of what you done for Jayleen Clouse." He'd walked to the far end of the room now and stood gazing out the window. "I saw that thingamajig y'all bought for the little one to sit in when she rides." He ran short fingers through his graying hair.

"I'm downright ashamed none of us here in Zell's Bush ever thought of doing such a thing."

"I didn't mean to make anyone feel badly."

"I'll fetch us something cold to drink," Etta Ann said, heading to the kitchen.

"We know that," Mr. Garwood said. He continued to pace the close quarters of the living room, his boots going soft and then loud as he stepped on and off the braided rug that spread out across the hardwood floor. An oscillating fan on the sideboard hummed, helping to move the warm air.

He paused for a moment. "I understand Tully may be clearing out of here come winter. Donna Dee told us about his studies. I been trying to help as much as I can by giving the boy extra jobs to do."

Silence fell again and Latina was uncomfortable. The afternoon was sultry. Few people in Zell's Bush had air conditioning and the Garwood's living room was stifling in spite of the fan. Latina wondered how she could politely slip away, but Mr. Garwood seemed intent on having this serious visit. She'd thought she could simply drop the paintings off and leave quickly. She never dreamed he would abandon the saws in the middle of the afternoon and come and visit with her.

"And another thing," Mr. Garwood went on as though he'd never stopped. "Etta and me, we been thinking about something. Before you came to Zell's Bush we never gave no thought to the little Clouse girl. We sorta felt they should keep her tucked away and let her just grow up best as she could. But now you come along and make us think there could be more to her life than just be hidden away."

Now it was Mr. Garwood's turn to be uncomfortable. Perspiration beaded on his forehead as he groped for words.

"What Parke is trying to say…" Etta Ann came to his rescue. Handing out the glasses of cold cider, she said, "We want to do more than just help Tully. Now that Donna Dee is leaving us—the last of our three girls—we thought it'd be nice to have someone else around. We want to build Jayleen and Althea a place right here." Etta Ann waved her arm toward the side of the house. "Out there on the ridge up from the garden would be a cozy spot for a house. That way we could look after them when Tully's away."

Mr. Garwood pulled a red handkerchief from his back pocket to wipe his brow. "We can't hardly expect Tully to return from college and settle down in that cabin for the rest of his life just because of his little sister."

Latina's heart was about to leap out of her chest. She struggled to keep her breathing and her voice even. "Do they know?"

"Not yet," Mr. Garwood answered. "In fact we just made our decision last evening after seeing the little one sitting so happy in that there fancy riding seat in Tully's pickup." He rubbed the stubble on his chin. "That really got to me."

Latina pressed her hands against the cold, wet glass of cider. If she'd been home she would have rubbed across her forehead. "Why are you telling me first?"

Etta Ann's round face beamed a wide smile. "Because you been the cause of it all. You opened our eyes."

"Aaron Clouse built their house." Latina's mind was racing. "Are you sure Jayleen will want to leave it?"

Mr. Garwood perched himself on the edge of the worn overstuffed chair, his elbows propped on his knees. "We're not sure. Not sure at all. All we can do is ask."

"May I…," Latina began, then wondered why she was even asking. This was none of her affair. She'd soon be leaving. "May I be the one to tell them of your offer?" She blurted it out quickly before she had a chance to change her mind.

Mr. Garwood shifted his gaze to his wife, then back to Latina. "I'd be much obliged if you would. I find it a hard thing to talk about." He heaved a deep sigh. "Now I'll write you a check for the paintings. You certainly earned it—in more ways than one."

The petunias in the old washtub in the Clouse's front yard were now a jungle of vivid pinks, orchids, and royal purples. Their gentle fragrance wafted toward Latina as she knocked at the front door. Her mind went back to the first night when she arrived here, soaking wet in Tully's arms. The petunias had been tiny green spikes.

Tully's pickup was parked in the yard, but it was Althea who pushed the screen door open. "Huw-wo Ah-teen-a. Wuv Ah-teen-a."

"When I saw it was you," Jayleen said from her rocking chair across the room, "I let her answer the door. Come on in."

Latina stepped inside and knelt to hold Althea close. She looked around wondering where Tully was.

"He's out checking the traps," Jayleen said with a knowing smile that made Latina blush. "Should be back any minute now. Come set a spell. I'm needing to ask a favor of you."

"Anything," Latina said, carrying Althea with her to the couch.

"Miss Wilkes has invited me to come to an all-day affair for parents of handicapped children next Friday in Springfield. We may not be back until quite late. I was wondering if Althea could spend the day with you."

All day? Jayleen trusted her to care for Althea for an entire day? "I'd love to have her. You know I would."

"Thanks so much." Jayleen's eyes were bright with excitement. "This is going to be a grand time for me. Meeting other folks who have the same problems to face as I do. I'm going to learn so much."

"You'll be the most well-adjusted one there," Latina said with a laugh. "They'll be asking you for advice."

Jayleen glowed under the compliment, but said in her usual way, "Oh pawsh."

"How will you get there?"

"Miss Wilkes is driving all the way up here to get me. Don't that beat all? I told her she didn't have to do that, but she wouldn't take no for an answer. She thinks I need to be at some group meetings like this. She also thinks…" Jayleen stopped then and studied the sock she was mending. "She also thinks since Tully's leaving, it might be good for me to find a place in Palatka to live where I'd be closer to people who could help me. She's even offered to help me find a little place."

"What did you tell her?"

Jayleen looked at her intently. "I'm a little mixed up right now. I want to do what's best for Althea, and I'm not sure being stuck away up here is the answer."

The slam of the back door announced Tully's return and sent Latina's heart pounding.

Althea jumped down out of Latina's lap and made a dash for her brother. He swooped down and caught her and lifted her toward the ceiling amid an explosion of giggles.

Then he sent a smile to Latina that she knew was meant for her alone. Some unspoken expression passed between them that was too deep for words. "Howdy, Latina."

"Hi. I was waiting for you to come in before I share the good news."

"Whoo-eee! You hear that talk, Althea? Good news! I'm all for that." He folded his tall frame into a nearby chair with Althea still nestled in his arms.

Latina hoped this news would be what they needed to hear. If Beverly had approached Jayleen about moving, it meant she'd already been considering making major changes in her life.

As briefly as possible, Latina told them of the Garwoods' offer to build a small house for Jayleen and Althea on the ridge above Etta Ann's garden. She explained that Parke Garwood wanted to do something to help Althea develop as much as was possible. And that he and Etta Ann wanted to help look after them now that both Donna Dee and Tully would be leaving.

The room grew quiet. Jayleen's rocker ceased its creaking. "That truly would be an answer to my prayers," she said with wonder in her voice.

Tully was shaking his head. "Garwood always was such a hard old bruiser. I never considered that he gave us a passing thought. A house by the sawmill. Sure would be handy, Mama. I reckon I could even help with it this fall before I leave in January."

"I wasn't sure you'd want to leave this house," Latina put in. "I know it's special to you."

"It is special, Latina," Jayleen agreed. "*Right* special, but so is Althea. I have to do what's best for her and her future."

Tully was still in a daze. "Close to other people," he said slowly. "Why you and Etta Ann'll be chatting all the time.

And whenever you feel like getting a cold soda pop you can walk up to Boles' and be there in a whipstitch."

Althea sensed something was in the air as she giggled and bounced on Tully's knees.

Latina felt it was time to leave and let mother and son work out all the details privately. As she excused herself and rose to go, Tully said, "Latina, I've been thinking. It's high time for us to have another picnic at the millpond—just you and me."

Latina felt warmth rise to her cheeks. No boy she'd ever know would have asked a girl for a date in front of his mother. "It is high time, isn't it," she said. "Exactly which high time did you have in mind?"

"My calendar tells me we won't have too many more Saturdays. How about this next one?"

Her throat went dry. Summer was nearly over. "This Saturday for sure," she said.

"I'll be at your house to fetch you at eleven."

"And," Jayleen added, "I'll have Althea there by eight on Friday morning. Miss Wilkes can pick me up from there."

"Saturday it is, Latina-Flower," Tully said.

When Latina told her parents of Mr. Garwood's offer to Tully's family her father was surprised. "Who would have thought that hard-nosed old businessman would do such an honorable thing? Wonder what made him think of it?"

"He said when he saw Althea so happy in that *thingamajig*, he realized she needed more than to be stuck away up in the hills alone."

Latina's mother was almost as excited about the whole thing as Jayleen had been. "It'll make life so much easier for Tully was well—knowing his family is safe and cared for while he's away at school."

"Do you think," Latina asked, struggling with her perplexing thoughts, "that life on campus will spoil Tully? He has such, such..." She groped for the right words. "Such golden qualities."

Her father gave his pipe a few soft puffs. "Tully's golden qualities, as you call them, run deep in that young man. I can't believe he will tarnish that easily. In fact, I think that others around him will bask in the reflected light of it. Right, Paulie?"

"I agree," her mother put in. "Tully will be a refreshing addition to Eagleton's student body."

They could bask in the reflected light of Tully's golden qualities, Latina thought, just as I do.

The ringing phone interrupted the conversation. It was Donna Dee.

"So you're not shopping late in Palatka tonight?" Latina asked. It seemed Donna Dee had been going non-stop ever since the wedding date was set.

"Not tonight. I came straight home from work. But on Friday, I have scads of things to do. Brad talked his daddy into letting me have the entire day off. Latina, can you drive me into Palatka on Friday? I just found out that Daddy and Mama need our car."

After checking with her parents, Latina assured Donna Dee she'd be available. "Oh, wait a minute!" She stopped suddenly, remembering. "I have to keep Althea all day Friday."

"Well, bring her along. She's no trouble."

Latina hesitated. The understanding was that Althea would be staying here at the house during the day. It didn't seem right to make other plans without letting Jayleen know. But since they didn't have a phone...

"I really need you," Donna Dee was saying on the other end. "Jayleen knows you'll take care of Althea no matter where you are."

"I suppose you're right. She loves to travel, that's for sure."

What busy week this was turning out to be, Latina mused as she replaced the receiver in its cradle. And crowning it all was her picnic alone with Tully on Saturday. She could hardly wait.

The car seat made transporting Althea infinitely easier, although noisier, as she made ample use of the squeaky horn hidden in the padded safety bar. At times, she remembered the horn on the steering wheel, and crying out, "Honk! Honk!" she strained to reach it.

Repeatedly, Latina spoke to her gently. "Althea's horn," she said patting the safety bar. Then, "Latina's horn," pointing to the steering wheel. "No, no. No touch Latina's horn."

Beaming, Althea would give her head a shake. "No, no," and honk her squeaky horn again.

Donna Dee laughed and plugged her fingers in her ears. "I hope my eardrums survive all these lessons," she said. Then added, "You do wonders with her, Latina. I've known her all her life and I never thought to try to teach her. I don't know how you do it."

"I'm not exactly sure either," Latina admitted, "it just seemed to come to me."

When Jayleen learned of the girls' plans to go into Palatka with Althea, she had agreed. "I trust the two of you fully and completely," she said, putting Latina's concerns at rest.

Late that afternoon, Donna Dee had only one more stop to make—that of the home of her future in-laws. She wanted to leave some parcels there as the Garwood home was becoming overcrowded with all her new acquisitions.

Latina and Althea waited in the car in front of the two-story home situated on the outskirts of Palatka. Presently, the bride-to-be came out to the car with a worried expression. "Latina, Mrs. Jenner's asthma is acing up, and Brad and his father are gone on a business trip for the night."

"I'm sorry to hear that. Is there anything we can do?"

"Well, if you don't mind awfully, I've offered to stay the night with her. Brad can bring me home tomorrow."

Latina didn't relish the thought of driving back to Zell's Bush alone with Althea, but confessing it would only make her friend feel bad. "Of course you stay with her, Donna Dee. She needs you."

"Thanks, Latina. You're an understanding dear. Please come in for a minute. I so want you to meet Mrs. Jenner."

Mrs. Jenner was a gracious hostess in spite of not feeling her best. She was kindly tolerant of Althea and overlooked falling cookie crumbs on the kitchen floor as they shared a snack.

Much of the conversation centered on the work of the law firm, and of course, the upcoming wedding, which left Latina somewhat out of the loop. She was anxious to get home before nightfall, so she excused herself as soon as possible.

Donna Dee walked her to her car and asked, "Latina would you mind stopping by the house and telling Daddy and Mama where I am? No sense in making a long-distance phone call from here."

"Sure. It's right on our way. Right, Althea?"

The little girl rocked back and forth in her car seat, anxious to be on the move again. She'd quickly become an avid traveler.

"Thanks again, Latina. How can I ever repay you for all you're doing for me?"

Latina settled herself behind the wheel. "Friends don't worry about paying back, do they?"

Donna Dee gave her arm a squeeze. "No, Latina, they don't."

When Latina drove out past the Palatka city limits, the sky held the last pink tints of daylight. She and Althea chattered to one another until at last, Althea lay her head on the padded bar and fell sound asleep.

It was dark by the time they reached Zell's Bush. Only the Coca-Cola sign in Boles' window and the bare bulbs glowing in front of the gas station gave hints of civilization. Latina wondered if Jayleen had returned home yet. She certainly hadn't planned to be this late getting home herself.

She noticed as she stopped the car by the sawmill that there were no lights on up at the house. Evidently, the Garwoods were still away. She'd have to leave a note on the door for them.

Switching on the car's interior light she rummaged in her purse for a scrap of paper and pen. Althea was still asleep. After she'd scribbled out the note, Latina looked up at the silent house perched on the ridge. She'd never seen it so dark and deserted. Shadows under the sheds gave them an eerie appearance.

Perhaps she could call the Garwoods later from her house. She switched the light off again and reached to turn the key in the ignition. But what in the world would Etta Ann think when she got home and Donna Dee wasn't there? She'd be needlessly frightened.

"This is foolishness," she chided herself sternly. "I'll run up there, fasten a note to the door and be on my way in no time. There's absolutely nothing to be afraid of."

Stepping from the air conditioned car, she was surprised to find the air sultry and still. A summer storm was brewing. The heavy smell of freshly cut wood hung thick in the air. She pushed the car door closed until it barely clicked so the slam wouldn't disturb Althea.

Her steps echoed as she walked up the winding path. In the distance, a whippoorwill cried. Ragged clouds swept by the moon. The front door screen was locked, but she was able to slip the note into the wooden screen door so that it was visible. She could only hope they'd see it. She could still call them later.

She made her way back down toward the car when a sudden movement under the big shed caught her eye.

"Hey there! Latina-Flower!"

She'd have known that high-pitched whining voice anywhere. It was Collier.

In an uncontrolled panic, she broke into a wild, frantic race for the car. As she did, his heavy footsteps sounded also, running from the sheds toward her. If only she could make it to the car and lock the door before he reached her.

The heat pressed in against her so that her lungs could scarcely function. A searing pain burned into her side. Her feet were barely touching the path. Collier's dark form was coming at her fast.

Absolutely terrified now, she grabbed at the partially opened door and flung herself into the seat. But he yanked at the door and pulled it from her grip before she could slam it in his face.

Chapter Twelve

"Now where're you going in such an all-fired hurry?" Collier asked.

Latina rubbed her sore fingers which had been entwined in the door handle as he forced it open. "Let go of the door, Collier. I've got to get Althea home. She's tired and Jayleen's expecting us."

The fracas had awakened Althea and at the sight of Collier she began to whimper.

"Hey there. You got the dimwit. Well, ain't this handy." He gave a lopsided grin. Roughly, he grabbed Latina's arm and tried to pull her out from behind the wheel. "Come out of there. I gotta talk to you."

"Leave us alone!" she cried out fighting against him. As she braced herself she thought of the keys and knew instinctively she must keep them from him. Twisting around, she managed to get her foot positioned to kick him hard. As she did, she slipped the keys out of the ignition and into her pocket.

He yelped at the kick and his anger only increased his strength. She felt herself being dragged from the car. She stumbled then caught her balance and stood frightened before him. His hand clenched her wrist. His dark eyes burned with anger.

"You ain't going nowhere, Latina-Flower. I need your help to get away. Tonight, I evened things up and now I got to get away from this place. I'm getting out of here for good."

"Evened things up? How?" Perhaps if she could keep him talking the Garwoods would drive up. Let them hurry, she prayed silently. Above all else she had to see that Althea was safe.

"Looky here." He pulled a wad of bills from his pocket. "Old man Garwood's office safe ain't too safe. This here makes up for all the times Tully got raises in pay and I didn't get none. And when he got extra jobs and I got nothing. It ain't fair that Tully's everybody's little pet and everybody hates old Collier."

So, she thought, he's robbed the mill office and now he's planning to run.

"That's not true, Collier." She forced a steadiness into her voice. "People like you, too."

With a quick strong jerk, he flipped her arm painfully behind her back and pulled her up against his chest. "Is that right, Latina-Flower? You're lying and you know it. You don't like me. You hate me. You knew I killed that stupid old coon and you hate me for it."

She wanted to scream *yes* in his face. She'd hated him from the first moment she'd laid eyes on him. Struggling, she tried to kick at his shins, but he pulled her arm tighter until she thought it would surely break. A groan escaped her lips, frightening Althea even more. The girl began to cry.

"Whatever you want me to do, Collier, I'll do it. But please let Althea go. You're scaring her."

"Aw, she don't know enough to be scared or not. And I got news for you, Miss Snooty City Girl, you're gonna do what I say no matter what. You're going to drive me away from this place where all these people hate me. They hated my daddy and my brothers, and now they hate me. I should have left long ago."

"I'll drive you anywhere. Just let me take Althea up to the house first…"

"Be quiet now! I got to get things figured out here."

As he spoke Latina sensed the pressure on her arm easing ever so slightly. With a burst of new strength, she wrenched from his grasp. She fished for the keys in her pocket and threw them as hard as she could into the brush at the edge of the clearing.

"Why you hare-brained dummy. Them keys was my way out of this dump."

Latina wanted to run, but there was no way she could leave Althea with this crazed guy. Glaring at her, Collier slowly reached down and slipped a knife out of his work boots. "This here's my skinning knife. I keep it sharper than my whittling knife. Now you get over there and find them keys."

She stared at the knife, remembering Coony's lifeless body lying on the blood-stained grass in their backyard. "It will take a long time to find them in the dark," she said, "and the Garwoods could drive in her any minute and catch you. Then what would you do?"

He snorted and cursed under his breath. "I don't need the likes of you nohow. All I need is one hostage to get me out of here. The dimwit'll do just fine. I know the hills like the palm of my hand and I'll walk out of here faster than spit on a hot skillet. You'll see."

Once again he grabbed her arm. "You come with me." He marched her ahead of him, with the knife still drawn, along the path through the dark tunnels of the sheds and into the moonlight on the other side. There before them stood the brick toolshed. Only the fear of his knife kept her from making a run for it.

"I need you to stay put so you can tell them I got me a hostage so if anybody comes after me or tries to stop me, I'll hurt the dimwit real bad. You hear?"

"No Collier!" she begged. "Not in there! I promise I won't leave! I'll stay right here."

"I can't trust nobody now." Keeping a tight hold on her, he fumbled with the bolted door, opened it and then shoved her roughly inside. The door slammed shut and she heard the padlock click.

She caught the sound of Althea's crying and calling her name, and managed to get hold of herself. If she listened closely she could tell the direction of his escape. Toward the woods on the far side of the road it seemed. But in the oven-like toolshed, filled with acrid odors of oil and grease, how could she trust her own senses? He might have taken her up into the hills behind the house.

On her feet now, she shoved her body against the door several times, but succeeded only in knocking the wind out of her. The shed was brick, but the door and its frame were of wood—old wood. Groping around for something to use to pound on the door, her hands met with a curtain of sticky cobwebs. When she located a long wooden handle that turned out to be a shovel, she used it to hit at the door. That too was useless. She could no longer hear Althea's cries. That terrified her more than the pitiful crying.

Thoroughly fatigued now, she sat down on the cool floor to wait. She mustn't panic. It couldn't be much longer before the Garwoods returned and Althea would be rescued. She hoped it wouldn't be too late.

Then she heard a faint cry in the distance. She strained to hear. It was a wail like that of a wounded animal.

She jumped to her feet again. She had to get out! Now that her eyes were accustomed to the dark, aided by open vents near the ceiling that let in dim moonlight, she spied a sledgehammer. If only she could lift it.

Straining at its weight, she groaned in an attempt to swing at the door near the point where the latch was situated. Nothing. Again came the eerie wailing cry.

If Collier had hurt Althea, she'd see to it he was put away forever.

It was the third swing of the heavy tool that finally loosened the latch and set her free. Instantly she was out and running, stumbling up the rutted drive, across the road and into the woods following the sounds of the cries. Now she knew it wasn't Althea who was hurt.

"Please help! Somebody help me!"

It was Collier.

"I'm coming," she called loud as she could. "Where are you? Althea? Althea? Where are you?"

Pushing through the underbrush in the darkness, she felt the briars clawing at her clothing and scratching her bare arms and face. At last, she could hear Althea's answer. "Ah-teen-ah! Ah-teen-ah!" Suddenly, Latina saw her coming over the ridge in her rolling gait.

Breaking into a run, Latina met the girl and lifted her into her arms, comforting her whimpers and pushing on through the trees. Collier's soft moans were just over the hill.

There on the floor of a low ravine he lay writhing in the damp leaves, his ankle caught in one of his own traps. His agonizing groans filled the air. "Oh, thank God, Latina. You came. Please, please help me. It hurts awful. Can't stand the pain. Please help me."

His own trap—and a big one. Not like the small one Dirk nearly stepped on. She looked at the bloody ankle and turned sharply away. She mustn't be sick.

"We'll go back to the mill and phone for help, Collier. I'll run as fast as I can."

"No! Oh no. Please don't leave me. I'm scared. Get it off me, Latina."

Remembering how Tully's strong hands struggled to open the one they found at the millpond she knew there was no hope of freeing him herself. "I can't Collier. There's no way I could open it." Her voice was soft and steady. She studied the chain securely fastened around a nearby oak tree. She wondered what he'd planned to trap with such a setup.

"I'm so scared," he said again, his eyes begging her.

Taking Althea by the shoulders and looking directly into her eyes, she instructed, "Althea, go to the car at the mill. To the car, Althea." She pointed in the direction of the sawmill. "Latina's horn! Latina's horn. Honk, honk!"

Althea's eyes brightened. With her thin hand, she mimed the honking, then laughed.

"That's right, Althea. That's a good girl. Honk Latina's horn and don't stop. Hold it and hold it. Now go!"

Althea headed off through the woods toward the sawmill.

Collier's groans had subsided somewhat. Probably going into shock. She moved closer, seated herself on the damp hollow of ground, lifted his head and laid it on her lap.

"I'm so sorry." His voice was low and raspy. "I wouldn't listen to Tully about the traps. I knew where everyone one of them was set, but I was running and forgot."

She tried to shush him, but he needed to talk.

"Tully tried and tried to tell me. But I wouldn't listen. I always knew it was wrong."

"Don't try to talk, just rest." She stroked his dark hair as though it were Dirk lying there.

Suddenly the car horn began to blare. And blare—without stopping.

"She's doing it ain't she?" he whispered. "How'd she know to do that?"

"That cousin of yours is one smart little girl, Collier."

"I never claimed her as kin before. Didn't want no dimwit for any kin of mine. I didn't know she could understand stuff."

"She sure can. And she can give out a lot of love, too."

Tears were coursing down his face now onto her soiled slacks. She wiped his face with the shirttail of her blouse.

Thunder rumbled behind them as Latina's eyes searched the darkness. Once again, he gave a low groan. "It hurts awful," he said.

"Squeeze my hand—hard." She placed her hand in his, allowing him to squeeze. It hurt, but she didn't care.

"It helps," he told her. "It really helps."

His young face was ivory against his black hair. How could she have ever been afraid of him? He was a hurt boy crying out for love and acceptance. Tully had seen it all along.

With eyes shut tightly, he gave another hard squeeze of her hand. Then he looked up at her. "How'd you get outta that toolshed?"

"Sledgehammer."

"Geez," he breathed. "You're really something." There was a long pause as his breathing evened out. Then, "You coulda left me." His words were barely audible now.

Latina then heard footsteps and voices in the distance. Help was on its way.

Tully reached her first, although she could tell by the commotion there were others following.

"Latina—you're safe!" He was by her side, his arms around her looking into her face, placing kisses on her forehead and cheeks.

"I'm fine, Tully, but your cousin her need a helping hand."

Latina had never seen Orville Boles move so fast, and to see him come galloping through the woods was comical in spite of the circumstances. Parke Garwood was right beside him.

The three men working together freed Collier from the wicked teeth of the trap. Orville and Parke gently carried the moaning boy back through the trees. Tully helped Latina up from the wet ground. She was gripped with a violent trembling that she'd resisted for many hours.

The first fat raindrops began to slap against the leaves and onto their hair and faces. Tully pulled off his shirt and placed it around her shoulders and held her close as they made their way out of the underbrush.

"Althea's all right?" she asked anxiously.

"She's with Etta Ann and she's fine. Proud of her honking job. I had just gone up to Boles' to watch for you when we heard it. Parke was pulling into the drive when Orville and I got here. Perfect timing."

Latina released a sigh that came from the innermost part of her.

In the Garwood's kitchen, Etta Ann wrapped Latina in a soft quilt and fixed her a cup of soothing hot tea. Collier had been placed in the Garwood's spare bedroom awaiting the ambulance to arrive from Palatka. Orville was by his side in an attempt to keep him comfortable as possible.

"You're in no condition to drive, young lady," Parke announced to Latina.

"I couldn't anyway," she told him. "I threw the keys into the brush to keep Collier from taking off."

Parke raised his shaggy eyebrows. "Quick thinking."

"Quick thinking for her to tell Althea to honk the car horn, too," Etta Ann added.

"Honk, honk!" Althea proclaimed grandly.

Tully rose to his feet. "I planned to take Latina with me and Althea anyway," he said. "I can bring her folks back to get their car later."

The noisy rainstorm had blown away, leaving behind a clean fragrance and a refreshing cool breeze. The threesome walked down the path to the pickup. One of Tully's arms held Althea, the other encircled Latina's shoulder.

"I'm sorry," he said to her. "By not stopping Collier, I nearly let the two of you get hurt." Gently placing Althea into her seat, he turned to take Latina in his arms, giving her the gentlest of kisses. Lifting her into the pickup beside Althea, he reached into his pocket, then took her hand. "Close your eyes."

Something small and smooth lay in her palm.

"Okay open."

It was miniature flower carved in careful detail from rose-hued wood. The exquisite beauty made her catch her breath.

"For my Latina-Flower." He cupped her hand in his and closed her fingers over the smooth wood. "Now let's get home. You and I have an important date tomorrow."

NORMA JEAN LUTZ

Norma Jean Lutz's writing career began professionally years ago when she enrolled in a writing correspondence course. Since then, she has had over 250 short stories and articles published in both secular and Christian publications. The full-time writer is also the author of over 50 published books under her own name and many ghostwritten books. Her books have been favorably reviewed in *Affair de Coeur, Coffee Time Romance, Romance Reader at Heart, and The Romance Studio* magazines, and her short fiction has garnered a number of first prizes in local writing contests.

Norma Jean is the founder of the Professionalism In Writing School, which was held annually in Tulsa for fourteen years. This writers' conference, which closed its doors in 1996, gave many writers their start in the publishing world.

A gifted teacher, Norma Jean has taught a variety of writing courses at local colleges and community schools, and is a frequent speaker at writers' seminars around the country. For eight years, she taught on staff for the Institute of Children's Literature. She has served as artist-in-residence at grade schools, and for two years taught a staff development workshop for language arts teachers in schools in Northeastern Oklahoma.

As co-host for the Tulsa KNYD Road Show, she shared the microphone with Kim Spence to present the Road Show Book Club, a feature presented by the station for more than a year. She has also appeared in numerous interviews on KDOR-TV.

Presently (in addition to her own writing endeavors) Norma Jean is actively reaching out to other writers via the Internet and social media.

If you are a newbie author and need help, look no further. Helpful information can be found on the Be A Novelist blog site. Why struggle out there all alone when you can benefit from Norma Jean's many decades of experience in the writing/publishing industry? Contact Norma Jean: normajean@beanovelist.com

OTHER TITLES
BY NORMA JEAN LUTZ

The Tulsa Series

The Tulsa Series is a four-title series of historical fiction that takes place against the backdrop of the infamous 1921 Tulsa Race Riot. Available on **Amazon Kindle** and **Barnes & Noble Nook**.

Tulsa Tempest

Tulsa Turning

Tulsa Trespass

Return to Tulsa

www.ingramcontent.com/pod-product-compliance
Lightning Source LLC
Chambersburg PA
CBHW060433130626
46555CB00005B/2339